CHEYENNE DRUMS

CHEYENNE DRUMS

Lewis B. Patten

Chivers Press • G.K. Hall & Co.
Bath, England   Thorndike, Maine USA

This Large Print edition is published by Chivers Press, England, and by G.K. Hall & Co., USA.

Published in 1999 in the U.K. by arrangement with Golden West Literary Agency.

Published in 1999 in the U.S. by arrangement with Golden West Literary Agency.

U.K. Hardcover   ISBN 0-7540-3848-3   (Chivers Large Print)
U.K. Softcover   ISBN 0-7540-3849-1   (Camden Large Print)
U.S. Softcover   ISBN 0-7838-8651-9   (Nightingale Series Edition)

The text of this Large Print edition is unabridged.
Other aspects of the book may vary from the original edition.

Set in 16 pt. New Times Roman.

Printed in Great Britain on acid-free paper.

British Library Cataloguing in Publication Data available

Library of Congress Cataloging-in-Publication Data

Patten, Lewis B.
    Cheyenne drums / Lewis B. Patten.
    p. (large print) cm.
    ISBN 0-7838-8651-9 (lg. print : sc : alk. paper)
    1. Cheyenne Indians Fiction. 2. Large type books. I. Title.
[PS3566.A79C49   1999]
813'.54—dc21
                                         99–22226

CHAPTER ONE

The sunwashed land lay flat, broken by an occasional low butte and sometimes by a dry wash or dry stream bed. No trees marred its flat expanse but there was brush—low sagebrush—and grass that drooped listlessly in the motionless air.

Dust arose from a distant speck that, as it came closer, resolved itself into a horse and man. A horse that ran steadily under the merciless goading of his rider's spurs. And a man whose face was set, whose mouth was hard, whose eyes burned with a fury that knew no respite.

He was a big man, and young. His broad shoulders and deep chest made him seem top-heavy for his mount. His hair was as black as the horse's gleaming hide and uncut for several weeks. A stubble of black whiskers made a bluish shadow on his jaw.

Behind him by almost twenty miles lay the Duer place—and Sally Duer, who had, with her spitefully jealous words, just ripped his world apart.

Why hadn't he guessed, he wondered furiously. Why hadn't he known, when everybody else in the country knew? Even his father must have known. Why, then, hadn't he spoken up? Before it came to this? Before it went this far?

His spurs raked the horse's sides cruelly. The animal gave forth a final burst of speed.

It lasted several minutes. Then the horse stumbled and fell, throwing his rider on ahead to fall, rolling, in the brush and grass.

The man got to his feet, his face gray with his fury. His eyes burned. He stared at the horse, lying on his side, hide covered with foam and sweat. He watched the animal's labored breathing and saw the angle of one of his forelegs.

With jerky movements, eloquent of both frustration and fury, Max Gleason yanked his revolver from the worn holster at his side. He fired once.

The horse jerked as the bullet struck. Then he was still. Max unbuckled the cinch and pulled the saddle off, nearly falling with the sudden release of the cinch from beneath the horse's body. He threw the saddle down, removed the bridle, and threw it down on top.

He stood for a moment then, staring first at the horse, then toward the north where the home place lay. At last he shifted his glance toward the west. He began to walk that way without glancing back. The Colfax place was at least seven miles from here, but it was closer than home. Besides, this had to be settled now.

He tramped along steadily. Under the steady rays of the sun he began to sweat. His fury did not cool.

The sun sank slowly toward the distant horizon ahead of him. It burned into his face until he tilted his hat forward against it. He stopped once to rest, rolled a wheatstraw cigarette, and puffed it angrily. Then he went on.

You hated something. You spent your life hating it. And then you found out a thing like this. He began to curse, softly, steadily.

And he remembered. However he tried not to remember, he couldn't help himself.

Nine he had been. Nine years old that fall of 1861. Old enough to ride with his father gathering the beef cattle that would be driven to Fort Laramie on the Platte.

They'd always gotten along with the Cheyenne. Once in a while they would turn over a beef to a wandering hunting party that had been unable to find any game. Or his mother would feed half a dozen painted braves in the yard just outside the kitchen door.

An uneasy truce, enforced by the presence of troops at Fort Laramie. But when the war threatened, the troops had been withdrawn. Or most of them had, leaving only a skeleton garrison. And the Cheyenne counted them as they were withdrawn.

From nearly ten miles away, Max and his father saw the smoke. They left the cattle when they did and spurred furiously toward the rising column.

Otto Gleason's face was white. His eyes were narrowed, his mouth a thin, straight line.

Young Max clung to his racing horse's back, occasionally glancing from the smoke to his father's tight-drawn face.

He learned fear of the Cheyenne during that endless ten mile ride. When they arrived at the smoking, blackened ruins of the house, he learned to hate as well.

The naked, bloody bodies of his mother and two sisters lay in the yard before the house. Their heads were as naked as their bodies where their scalps had been yanked away. Huge, blue-green flies covered their bloody scalps.

Grotesquely positioned, like dolls tossed down by a child who is through with them. Max's young stomach cramped, knotted, and emptied itself all over one side of his horse. He fell off the animal, weak, sweating but cold with his horror and his fear.

His father stripped the saddle from his horse and covered his mother's body with the saddle blanket. He gathered up the little girls, one after the other, and laid them at her side, afterward covering them with his shirt. Naked to the waist, he poked around in the ruins of the barn until he found a shovel with at least part of the handle left. Then he began to dig.

Young Max retched and retched until nothing more came up. He wished he could cry, but his eyes were dry. He kept looking around fearfully as though the murder party of Cheyennes might reappear.

His father finished the graves in utter darkness. He laid the bodies of his wife and daughters in them, muttered a few words of prayer, and filled them in. He collapsed in exhaustion on the ground, but he did not sleep. Nor did young Max sleep. He stared into the night fearfully, chilled and trembling.

When morning came, Otto Gleason took the trail of the Cheyennes. He took young Max along because there was nothing else to do with him. And Max accompanied him in terror, hating the Indians for what they had done, but also praying silently that his father would not catch up with them.

He learned shame because fear overpowered his hatred and outrage. And because of the shame, he hated more strongly than before.

The trail led away westward and lost itself in the mixed trails of a village that had moved only hours before. Because he knew he could not fight an entire village, Otto Gleason turned back helplessly.

Remembering as he walked, Max felt the old coldness in his spine, the fear that had stayed with him for months, making him wake in the night, crying out his fear.

Vaguely he understood that not all his hatred of the Cheyenne had been caused by the murder of his mother and sisters. Part of it was caused by what they had done to him.

He also understood that, in this respect, he was different from his father. His father hated

5

—bitterly and vitriolically. But it was pure hatred, uncolored by any trace of fear.

The sun dropped to the horizon, hung poised there for several moments before it sank slowly out of sight. Briefly it stained the few scattered clouds orange and gold. Then even this light faded and deep gray stole across the land.

Max Gleason plodded along stolidly. The night's chill did not touch him. His body was heated by his emotions, and by the exertion of walking.

Damn her! Damn Marian Colfax. She knew. She must know. And yet she'd let him go on seeing her, knowing how he felt.

She had let him propose marriage, and she must have been laughing inside all the time he did. Worst of all, she had accepted him.

But thank God he hadn't married her. Thank God he'd found out in time. If he hadn't . . .

Hell, he'd have had Indian babies in his house. And the whole countryside would have laughed at him. Max Gleason, who hated Cheyennes worse than the Lord hated sin. Max Gleason, with a passel of Indian kids. He shuddered visibly.

The sky darkened and turned wholly black. Stars winked out. A glow grew behind Max above the eastern horizon, and after a while a huge, yellow moon poked its rim above the plain. Still he walked, but he was drawing closer now. And with the narrowing of the distance between himself and the Colfax place, his fury steadied down to a bright, cold flame.

He had no plans as to what he would do when he reached the place. All he wanted at the moment was to face her, and curse her, and leave again.

He saw the light ahead while he was still a quarter-mile away. His pace increased to a swift shamble. His hands began to shake.

He burst into the house without bothering to knock. Marian Colfax turned from where she was standing at the stove. She stared at him bewilderedly. 'Max! What's the matter? What's happened to you?'

He glared at her, face sweating, hands trembling. He licked his lips, and his voice came out like a hoarse croak. 'Bitch. You dirty Indian bitch!'

Her face whitened. 'Max! What . . . ?'

He crossed the room to her. One of his hands went out, seized her dress at the throat, and ripped it savagely. Her undergarments still covered her so his hands went out again, almost frantically.

Stunned at first, Marian now began to struggle. But it was no use. He ripped her clothes from her body, sometimes almost shredding them. She screamed, and wept, but there was no one to hear.

He saw darkness in her skin because that was what he wanted to see. He stripped every

7

shred of her clothing off, and then, because he was still unsatisfied, began to strike her methodically with his fists.

He knocked her to the floor amid the pots and pans and broken dishes scattered during the struggle. Then he stood over her and cursed her in terms so foul that she covered her ears with her hands.

He was shaking now, and cold. He turned suddenly and stalked out of the house, leaving the door gaping wide.

He shambled across the yard to the corral. He caught a horse and, with trembling fingers, fashioned a hackamore out of a piece of rope. He leaped to the horse's back and spurred away.

Half a mile from the house, he yanked the horse to a halt. His stomach churned with nausea. He retched, and gagged, and vomited all over one side of the horse.

And it was once again as it had been nearly twenty years ago. The stink. The memory of nakedness and blood. The fear that mingled with hatred until it was like a mortal sickness in his mind.

He spurred the horse on toward home. There would be consequences for what he had done tonight, but he didn't think of that. He was like a man in a stupor, in whom there is no thought.

*   *   *

Behind him, in the kitchen of the Colfax house, Marian stirred and, only barely conscious, struggled to her knees. She became aware of her nakedness and pulled herself to her feet, using a table for support. She saw the open door and stumbled from the room into the dark part of the house beyond.

From the darkness came sounds like the sounds of a wounded animal. Incoherent sounds that continued for a long, long time before they became the weeping sounds of a woman who has been hurt.

She returned to the kitchen, a flannel wrapper covering her. She got down the tub and placed it in the center of the floor. She dumped water into it from the kettles on the back of the stove.

She bathed, her face filled with stunned revulsion, scrubbing herself hard with strong soap. She put on the wrapper when she had dried herself.

Carrying the lamp, she went into her bedroom and stared into the mirror over her dresser. She pulled the wrapper aside and stared at her body, marked now with red blotches from Max's fists.

Indian, he had called her. Indian bitch. What had he been talking about? What had he meant?

Her trembling returned. She picked up the lamp, nearly dropping it. She used both hands to hold it and returned to the kitchen like a

9

sleep walker. She sat down in a kitchen chair and stared emptily at the wall. She was still sitting there when her brothers returned at midnight.

They were medium-sized men. Ben, the oldest, was six years older than Marian. Ed was two years older than she.

Ben wore a long, rusty, cavalry style mustache. Ed was clean-shaven, but tonight he needed a shave. They trooped toward the house, yelling, laughing, but they turned silent as they stepped through the kitchen door.

Ben stared at the wreckage in the room. He stared at his sister, still sitting in the kitchen chair staring blankly at the wall. He stared at the tub in the middle of the floor.

He saw the finger marks on her arms and throat. He saw the bruise beneath her left eye and the scratch across her forehead. His face whitened and his eyes blazed. He crossed the room and seized her shoulders. 'Who?' he asked in a voice so soft it could scarcely be heard. 'Who was it?'

She did not reply.

He shook her violently. His fingers bit into her shoulders, as Max Gleason's had done. She shrank away from him.

He released her. He snatched another chair and sat down facing her. His hands were clenched into fists so tight the knuckles were white. But his voice was surprisingly soft. 'Sis, you tell us who it was. We got to know. We got to get the bastard before he hurts someone else.'

She turned her head and stared dumbly at him. She swallowed several times before she spoke. 'He said Indian. He said I was a dirty Indian bitch.'

Ben's body seemed to freeze, without motion. Marian asked, 'Why did he say that?'

'Because ma . . .' He stopped suddenly. He asked again, 'Who was it, sis? You tell me now. Please.'

A little sanity came briefly to her eyes. 'Tell me first why he said that.'

'Will you name him if I do?'

She nodded wordlessly. Something new seemed to come into her eyes, as though she feared what she would hear.

Ben said hoarsely, 'It's a lie anyway, so I don't see no reason for not tellin' you. Ma was captured by the Cheyenne. It was after that when she had you. If was after she came home.'

Marian was silent, so after a moment he asked, 'Now who was it, sis? You said you'd tell me who it was.'

Her voice was the merest whisper. 'It was Max. It was Max Gleason, Ben.'

Ben's eyes narrowed and his mouth became a thin, hard line. He said, 'Get some horses, Ed. And hurry up.'

CHAPTER TWO

Ed, whitefaced, left the room and disappeared into the darkness. Marian said, 'No!' She looked up, the stunned apathy disappearing momentarily from her face. 'No, Ben. You're not to go over there.'

'Not go over there? Are you crazy? You think we're just going to let a thing like this go?'

'You've got to. If you go over there, you'll kill him. And you'll hang for murder. Both of you.'

'Not when the sheriff knows what he did to you.'

Her expression became pleading. 'Ben, that's what I don't want anyone to know. Can't you see?'

A shadow of doubt crossed his face. She said, 'Please, Ben. You know what people will do with something like this. I'll leave. I'd have to leave.'

'The hell you would!' He went to the door and bellowed into the darkness, 'Hurry up, Ed!'

Marian's face was still and cold when he turned to face her again. She said softly, 'Ben, if you go over there tonight, I'll be dead when you get back.'

The doubt returned to his face. His eyes

took on a worried, baffled look. He knew his sister, and he knew she would do whatever she said she would. He said pleadingly, 'Marian, please. Don't talk like that.'

'I mean it, Ben.'

Ed appeared in the door. 'I got the horses, Ben.'

Ben stared at his sister's face. He glanced uncertainly at Ed. Ed asked, 'What're you waitin' for? Let's go.'

'We ain't going, Ed. Not tonight, at least.' He turned his head toward Marian. 'He's going to pay for this. One way or another, he's going to pay.'

He hesitated a long time, studying Marian's face. His expression was one of baffled fury. At last he said, 'Put one of the horses up. Take the other and go after the sheriff. By God . . .' He left the sentence dangling.

Marian did not look up. Ed glanced from his sister to Ben and back again. Then he withdrew from the door. Several moments later, his horse's hoofs made a dull racket as he rode away toward town.

Marian relaxed visibly. Her hands went up and covered her face. Sudden sobs shook her body.

Ben knelt beside her and put his arms around her awkwardly. He held her this way, silently, until her sobs had subsided somewhat. Then he got up and began to pace the floor.

Marian's voice was soft. 'How do you know

13

it's a lie, Ben? How do you know?'

He yanked his head around. 'I just know! You ain't got no Indian blood. Any damn fool can see that just by lookin' at you.'

'But how can you be sure? If she was kidnaped by the Cheyennes . . . if she was with them any time at all . . .'

'It's a lie, that's all!' His voice rose angrily. 'Ma would of fought 'em.'

'I know that, Ben. I know she would. But maybe . . . maybe anyway, no matter how she fought . . .'

His face set angrily. Jaws clenched, he grated, 'You stop that kind of talk! It didn't happen! Not to ma.'

She asked, 'You're older than me, Ben. You must have been old enough to remember things when she was taken. When was it? How long was she gone?'

He scowled furiously. Marian insisted, 'What time of year? What month?'

'Just before Christmas. December, it must've been.'

Her eyes were wide, sparkling with tears. 'Are you sure, Ben? My birthday's in August. That would mean . . .' She stopped and her face took on a lifeless look. 'I guess it wouldn't mean anything, would it? If it was December they took her. She could have been . . . before . . . or afterward . . . Ben, it wouldn't prove a thing.'

'Maybe it was some other month,' he

14

growled. He paced back and forth furiously for several minutes. When he turned, his eyes burned. 'She'd have fought 'em off for a long time. So that proves . . .'

'I fought Max too, Ben. But it didn't help.'

He whirled. 'What the hell are you tryin' to do? Prove that what Max said was true? It ain't, I tell you. You're white. You're all white just the same as me!'

She got up silently and went into the dark part of the house. He stared at the door helplessly. After a while he heard her bed creak, and a few moments after that heard her crying again.

He ought to have gone to Gleason's anyway, he thought. She wouldn't have killed herself. She had too much sense.

But he was no more sure now than he had been before. He walked to the door and stared angrily into the night.

*   *   *

Mart Leathers sat in the sheriff's office with his booted feet up on the desk. He stared idly at the scars in the desk made by the sheriff's spurs. Sam Farley had been sheriff almost twenty years. In twenty years a single pair of spurs can wear away a lot of solid oak.

It was late and he knew he ought to go to bed. But he didn't move. He was thinking that this whole damned country was going to blow

15

sky high when its inhabitants found out what he and the sheriff already knew—that a mistake had been made in the original survey of the Cheyenne reservation thirty miles north of town, that the new survey put the line almost ten miles this side of the original boundary.

He frowned worriedly. It was only a matter of time until they did find out about it. And when they did . . .

They were using that strip of land. Those whose ranches bordered it, and one or two others were using it for grazing land. Giving it up to the hated Cheyenne would be unthinkable. Particularly for some of the older ones, who had been here twenty years ago at the time of all the Indian trouble. Those old ones knew how to hate and some of them had plenty of reason for their hate.

Otto Gleason for instance. His wife and two daughters had been murdered and scalped by the Cheyenne. Clem Heller—the girl he was going to marry had been killed in a stagecoach attack while she was on her way to him. Joe Duer—he still limped from a Cheyenne arrow wound. And the Colfax family—Sam, Ed, and Marian—their mother had been kidnaped and held for months by the Cheyenne.

All these families, except the Duers, bordered the strip that would, eventually, be declared part of reservation land. All of them used it for grazing land. And every one of

16

them would fight. Maybe in the courts at first. But if they got no relief in the courts, they'd fight in the Cheyenne villages too. They'd fight any way they had to fight.

Over the faint sounds of revelry in the late-closing saloons, he heard the pounding of a horse's hoofs on the hard-packed street at the north end of town. He lifted his head as the sounds came closer.

The horse pulled up, plunging, in front, lifting a cloud of dust that drifted through the open door. He removed his feet from the desk and swung the swivel chair around.

Ed Colfax burst through the door. His eyes were wild, his face flushed. He asked breathlessly, 'Where's Sam Farley?'

'In bed at home. It's his night off. What's the matter?'

Ed stared at him almost blankly for a moment. He said hesitantly, 'Ben said to get the sheriff.'

'I'll take care of it. What's wrong?'

'Well, I guess . . .' Ed Colfax took a deep breath. 'It's that son-of-a-bitch, Max Gleason. He come over to our place tonight while Ben an' me was gone . . . Well, God damn him, he abused Marian. Ripped all her clothes off an' beat her up with his fists. Ben said to come after the sheriff, but by God what we oughta done was go over there an' kill the bastard. Maybe I'll do it yet.'

He stopped, out of breath. Mart felt an icy

17

coldness in his chest, one that seemed to restrict his breathing. He suddenly wanted to kill, but he wanted more than that. What he really wanted was to feel Max Gleason under his hands, to . . .

He took a long, slow breath. His eyes were narrowed, his mouth a thin line. Ed stared at him, for an instant sobered by his expression.

Mart reached for his hat, lying on the desk. He crammed it on. He said, 'Get down to the stable and have Eben saddle me a horse. I'll walk down.'

Ed still stared at him dumbly. Mart's voice was like a whip. 'Move!'

Ed turned and hurried out the door. The sound of his horse's hoofs diminished as he rode toward the stable.

Mart blew out the lamp. Going toward the door, he snatched a rifle from the rack. He slammed the door behind him, fighting to control the fury that threatened to consume him.

Marian! Oh, good God, why had it had to be Marian? He strode toward the stable furiously, a sick, nauseous feeling in his stomach, a feeling of lightness in his head. Maybe by the time he reached Gleason's place he'd have cooled off some—enough to keep him from killing Max. And maybe he wouldn't have cooled off at all.

He'd courted Marian himself, at the same time Max Gleason had been courting her.

18

Maybe if Sam Farley hadn't sent him south to Yuma with that prisoner ... Maybe if he hadn't been gone so long ... But he had. And when he'd returned Farley had told him that Marian and Max Gleason were engaged.

He hadn't seen her since. But he could see her in his mind plainly enough. He would always see her, he supposed. Tall and straight and proud. And her eyes ... eyes that a man could drown in. Her laughing mouth. The line of her throat ... Her wonderful dark brown hair ...

He realized that he was cursing savagely beneath his breath. Max Gleason had hurt her, stripped her, beaten her with his fists. The man was a mad dog that had to be killed!

He reached the stable. Ed sat his fidgeting horse beside the door. Eben Rayburn came out, leading a saddled horse. Mart took the reins and swung astride. He raked the animal savagely with his spurs.

The horse thundered down the street toward the edge of town. Ed Colfax raced to catch up, but he did not catch up until they were more than a mile from town. When he did, Mart turned his head and yelled, 'Why? For God's sake, why?'

For several moments Ed did not reply. Mart shouted, 'Damn you, why'd he do it?'

'You won't tell ... ?'

'Hell no, I won't tell! You know better than to ask me that!'

19

'He said she was Injun. He said because ma was taken by the Cheyenne . . .'

Mart uttered a single, savage expletive. He roared, 'Any damn fool can see . . .'

There was no doubt in his mind. But even if there had been, even if he'd known Marian was half Indian, it wouldn't have made any difference to him. With Max, though, hatred of the Cheyenne was an obsession.

Understanding why Max had done what he had didn't lessen Mart's fury. What he'd done was unforgivable. And he'd pay for it. One way or another, he'd pay for it.

The miles fell slowly behind the racing pair. The horses sweated, and lathered, and at last Ed's began to lag. Mart yelled, 'I'll go on. You slow down or you won't have a horse.'

Ed Colfax didn't reply. His horse fell gradually behind.

Mart welcomed the solitude. He was better able to think. He couldn't storm over to Gleason's and kill Max. He was a sheriff's deputy. He was sworn to uphold the law, not to break it or take it into his own hands. He tried to force his thoughts from that fact, but it kept intruding however he tried not to let it intrude.

He could arrest Max though. He could haul him into town and throw him into jail. He could bring him to trial for assault . . .

He shook his head almost angrily. A trial would mean that Marian would have to testify.

20

Max's accusation that she was half Indian would come out. So would the details of what he had done to her.

Was that what Ben Colfax wanted? He shook his head in puzzlement. He couldn't believe it. Not of Ben.

Killing Max wouldn't be any different, he admitted reluctantly. Ben and Ed would have had to stand trial for murder. And everything that had happened would have come out anyway.

There was only one way to handle this. Maybe that way was best anyway.

His face was grim as he hauled his horse in at the Colfax house. He dropped the reins and stalked to the house.

Ben Colfax opened the back door. A lamp was still burning inside the kitchen even though the sky was gray with approaching dawn. Mart went inside.

Ben reached for the coffee pot. His hand trembled slightly. He poured Mart a cup of black coffee before he said, 'Ed tell you what happened?'

Mart nodded. 'How is she? Is she all right?'

'I could hear her cryin' until ten minutes ago.'

Mart asked coldly, 'What do you want me to do?'

It was a long time before Ben answered him. 'I don't know, Mart. I'm damned if I know what I want you to do. Ed and me was

21

going over there last night. I'd of killed him.'

'What stopped you?'

'Marian. She said if we went over and killed Max that she'd be dead when we got back. Hell Mart, I couldn't risk it, the way she was, hysterical and everything. She might have done it. She might have killed herself.'

'You want me to haul him into jail?'

Ben Colfax shook his head. 'Hell no, I don't want that. You'd have to charge him and bring him to trial. The whole damn business would come out.'

Mart said, 'You sit tight. I'll go over there.' He lifted the coffee cup and drained the last of it. He noticed that his own hand was shaking.

And why not? His feelings toward Marian hadn't changed. They would never change. Anybody that hurt her ... He got up and went to the kitchen door. The door leading to the rest of the Colfax house was ajar slightly. He had a sudden feeling that Marian was there, just beyond that door, watching him, listening.

She wouldn't want to talk to him right now. But in a day or two ... He was coming out here again. Maybe if he was patient and persistent enough ...

He went out into the chill of coming dawn. He swung to his horse's back. He pointed the animal northeast toward the Gleason ranch.

CHAPTER THREE

Mart Leathers rode steadily, pushing his horse but rationing out the strength left in him over the span of miles he had to go. Gleason's place was about twelve miles from Colfax's and it was another twelve or thirteen back to town.

The sky grew lighter and the rising sun lifted off the horizon like a blazing gold balloon. It climbed across the sky, warming the dewy land, warming too the man who pushed his horse steadily northeast.

He was a tall young man, twenty-five on his last birthday. His shoulders were broad and muscular beneath his thin blue cotton shirt. His gun rode low against his thigh but was not tied down. Sam Farley, who had taught him to shoot, always said, 'There's fast-draw men around. Plenty of them. They most always miss with their first shot, and the man who wins is the one who puts a bullet in the other first. You learn to shoot straight with your first shot and you needn't be afraid to face the best of 'em.'

Mart's hair was the color of the drying grass that covered this section of Wyoming plain. Over his jaws a light stubble of the same color showed. His eyes were blue—a blue that could be cold as ice, but a blue that could be laughing and friendly too.

Sam Farley wasn't going to approve of him today, he thought. Sam was a stickler for law. But Sam also had a high regard for women in general, for Marian Colfax in particular. He might not approve, but he sure as hell wasn't going to condemn.

The first white-heat of fury was gone from Leathers now. But the coals of rage still smoldered in his mind. Sight of Max Gleason would fan them like a wind, he knew. He dropped a hand to the revolver, at his side, hesitated, then withdrew the gun and, turning halfway around in his saddle, dropped it in one of his saddlebags. If he didn't have a gun, he couldn't kill. If he did . . . no telling what might happen when he finally faced the man who had manhandled Marian last night.

Each landmark he knew passed behind him with maddening slowness. But at last he brought the Gleason place in sight.

The big, two-story, white frame house. The white picket fence that surrounded the front yard. The profusion of flowers grown there by Della Chavez who had been the Gleasons' housekeeper for as long as Mart could recall.

And out in back, the enormous barn, whose roof was sagging now. The corrals. The other buildings and the rusty graveyard of haying machinery.

North of the buildings stretched the hay meadows, up a long draw that carried Cheyenne Creek in its center. Some of the stacks were brown, like great, fat loaves of bread. Some were green, having just been put up.

On the porch of the house sat Otto Gleason, rocking away the last years of his life, bound to the chair by two crippled legs smashed years before by a falling horse. Mart rode directly to the porch and stared at Gleason angrily. 'Where's Max?'

The old man shrugged, and stared at Mart with penetrating eyes that had lost none of their sharpness. He was thin, this old man, but his thinness was that of a piece of ancient rawhide. His skin, stretched tight over the backs of his two hands resting on the arms of the chair, was like parchment and lightly freckled. His hair was snowy white, worn long on the back of his neck. He had a mustache that resembled the one Ben Colfax wore except that it was also white. The whiteness of hair and mustache was in sharp contrast to his face, browned almost to the color of mahogany.

Mart stared at the house. Max had been up all night. He was probably asleep. He roared, 'Max!'

The old man said, 'You after Max? Got a warrant for him?'

Mart shook his head. He saw a curtain in an upstairs window stir. And suddenly all his white-hot fury returned. He yelled, 'Max! Get your ass down here!'

Otto Gleason asked, his voice suddenly very sharp, 'What's he done?'

'Ask him.'

'I'm askin' you. And don't get smart with me, neither!'

Mart glanced at the old man's face. The eyes were like bits of stone. He said, 'He abused Marian Colfax last night. Ripped off her clothes and beat her up.'

'Raped her, you mean?'

Mart turned blazing blue eyes on him. He'd been avoiding that question in his mind all night. Just the thought of it turned his insides to ice and made his hands tremble violently.

He heard the screen door slam. Max stood on the porch in front of it. He was fully dressed, but his hair was touseled and uncombed. There was a raw scratch on his right cheek, another above his left eye.

He glanced at Mart, looked away, and then stared at the condemning eyes of his father. In spite of his twenty-eight years, he suddenly was as defensive as a small boy. 'She's a goddam Injun, Pa. She's half Injun.'

Mart suddenly could stand no more. With a wordless sound deep in his throat, he left his saddle, nearly falling when he reached the ground. He vaulted over the porch rail and charged at Max like a maddened bull.

Max snatched for his gun, but his father's voice cut the silence like a whip, 'Put it up! He ain't got no gun!'

Mart struck him with his shoulder, bowling him back, staggering, the length of the porch. Max crashed against the rail at the end of the porch, taking out a twelve-foot section of it. He fell on his back in a flower bed, and Mart landed on top of him. The gun skidded along the porch floor nearly to the old man's feet.

The old man bent and tried to reach it, but was short by almost a foot. He began to hitch his chair toward it.

The screen door banged open, and Della Chavez came onto the porch. She glanced at the two in her flower bed and screeched, 'Get up out of there before I brain you both!' She advanced toward them, a heavy skillet in her hand.

Mart's first blow landed squarely on Max's nose. It seemed to burst like a ripe tomato, splashing blood all over his face. He squirmed and struggled, trying to roll beneath Mart's weight, trying to avoid Mart's second blow.

He failed. The blow landed on his mouth. But now he brought up his knees and straightened with a whiplash movement that flung Mart off.

Max struggled to his feet. Mart was rising too, and Della was still screeching at them from the edge of the porch. Max stared at the deputy for an instant, then turned and lunged away. He ran shamblingly toward the barn.

Mart followed. He caught Max with a flying leap just short of the corral, but Max got his

27

hands on the lower pole. Using it for leverage, he yanked his legs out of Mart's grip.

He climbed the fence and jumped down on the other side. Mart followed, landing on top of him and knocking him down again into the litter of dry manure inside. The dozen or so horses inside the corral snorted and plunged away from the fighting pair.

Back on the front porch Otto Gleason roared helplessly, unable now to see what was going on. From the barn, from the bunkhouse, from the blacksmith shop, the hands began to gather to watch the fight.

Max got up, hesitated briefly between running again and standing to fight. He elected to stand and fight, but he couldn't stand against the maddened fury in Mart. Mart's wildly swinging fist caught him on the ear and drove him helplessly backward, staggering, directly into the frightened horses on the far side of the corral.

He fell, and they plunged over him, now crowding along the fence to get away to the far side of the corral. Miraculously not a hoof touched Max.

He got no chance to rise. Mart was on him again, swinging his fists with a wild disregard for his own defense. In desperation, Max got a handful of dry manure and flung it directly into Mart's face.

Blinded, Mart turned his head. He knuckled his eyes, trying frantically to clear them. Max rolled him off, rose, and stood above him, kicking him savagely—in ribs, face, chest, stomach.

Mart covered by hugging himself with his arms and bringing up his knees. Sharp pains shot through his body. His eyes burned like fire, streaming tears that mingled with and streaked the dry manure on his face.

Rolling away in desperation, he realized that the tears had partly cleared his eyes. He banged against the corral fence, and pulled himself upright.

Max followed him, swinging wildly and ferociously. Mart ducked, and one of Max's fists slammed solidly into one of the corral poles.

He howled with the pain of it. And Mart took the offensive from him.

Again he drove Max across the corral, his eyes streaming tears and rimmed with red. Again Max fell among the plunging, terrified horses on the other side.

This time one of them stepped on his leg. He got up, limping now, looking around for some weapon he could use to end the fight.

There was a pitchfork leaning against the poles, but it was on the outside. He reached through between the poles and got the handle in both hands.

Mart's fist slammed into the back of his neck, driving his face against the poles. He stood there shaking his head numbly a moment, then fell back, bringing the sharp-tined fork with him. He swung around, groggy and staggering, and lunged at Mart with the fork.

One tine took Mart in the thigh, penetrating deep. The pain of it was maddening, the more so because he could see how rusty and filthy the fork was.

His eyes still burned fiercely from the dry manure, but he could see. He could see and his rage was unappeased.

He reached down and seized the forkhandle with both hands. He yanked it free, then yanked it savagely out of Max Gleason's hands. For the briefest instant he hesitated, fork poised. Then he flung it aside and rushed once more.

The pain in his thigh was a steady fire. His leg threatened to give out with each step he took. But he followed Max across the corral, each swing wild, but each connecting with some part of Max's face.

He smashed Max's nose, which was already smashed. He drove his fist into Max's mouth and felt teeth give before his bloody knuckles. He raised a blue welt as big as a walnut on Max's cheekbone.

Max went down and Mart straddled him, pounding with single-minded concentration until Max's body went limp beneath his own. And still he pounded, until a couple of the hands jumped down from the top rail of the corral and pulled him off.

When they released him, he nearly fell. He stumbled to the fence and hung on, head reeling, vision blurring, lungs working like a gigantic bellows.

He was covered with blood and dirt. Somewhere he could hear a voice yelling frantically. It was a while before he understood, before he recognized it as Otto's voice.

He shambled to the corral gate and opened it. He closed it behind him and limped slowly back toward the house. He looked at Otto, sitting red-faced and helpless on the porch.

He walked to his horse without speaking. He tried three times before he made it to the saddle.

He looked down at Otto Gleason for a moment. Then, still without speaking, he turned the horse and rode away. Behind him he could hear the old man grumbling and could hear Della scolding from the flower bed where she was kneeling to repair the damages.

He should have felt satisfied, but he did not. He hadn't beaten Max nearly as badly as he'd wanted to.

His head reeled. His leg throbbed regularly. He'd have to find Doc Williams as soon as he got back to town and have it taken care of. A wound like that could cause blood poisoning. It could cost him his leg if he neglected it.

He remembered, suddenly, the look that

had been on Max Gleason's face as he smashed his fist into the unyielding wood of the corral pole. And he grinned slowly to himself with the memory.

Several times on that ride back to town his consciousness faded. Or else he dozed. He could not tell which. But each time he would awake with a start, conscious first of the pain in his thigh, next of the uncounted hurts in his body and face.

But at last, near noon, he saw it ahead of him.

He rode first to the sheriff's office. Sam Farley was sitting on the bench in front of it. Sam stood up and came to the side of his horse, his face filled with concern. 'What in God's name happened to you?'

'Tell you later. Right now I want to see Doc.'

'Need any help?'

'I'll make it all right.' He touched his horse lightly with his spurs and moved on down the street.

He drew rein before a tiny, boxlike house set far back from the street where a weathered sign hung. You could read it only if you already knew what it said, 'J. F. Williams, M.D.' He swung laboriously from his horse, pulled a rein through the ring on the lion's head hitching post, and dropped the loop of it over the rusty lion's head.

He opened the gate and limped up the walk.

He could smell himself, the horse manure, the sweat . . . He raised the knocker on the door and let it fall.

Doc opened the door, squat, graying, running to paunch these days. A pair of gold-rimmed glasses were pinched to his nose.

He saw the blood on Mart's pants immediately and asked, 'You shot?'

Mart shook his head. 'Pitchfork tine.'

'That's a damsite worse. Come in and let's get after it.'

CHAPTER FOUR

Frowning worriedly, Sam Farley stared after his deputy. He watched Mart dismount stiffly and limp through the gate toward Doc Williams' house.

Spread-legged, he seemed to be rooted in the street, like one of the gigantic old cottonwoods at the edge of town. He wondered if news of the new survey had gotten out. He wondered if that trouble had begun.

He began to walk slowly toward Doc's place.

There was something permanent about Farley. He had been sheriff of Pawnee County for more than twenty years. He had been here at the time of the Indian troubles in '61. He had been with the cavalry troop that rescued

Sarah Colfax from the Cheyenne.

Nearing sixty, his hair was as white as that of Otto Gleason. His face had the same mahogany color from endless years of burning sun, of howling winter wind, of glare on the land when it was covered with winter's snow and ice.

He carried the scar of a Cheyenne arrow in his chest. He carried the bullet scars of half a dozen wounds. But he had something else that few men ever achieve—a kind of personal power that sprang from his indomitable will, from his unthinking, almost instinctive courage, from his unquestioning faith in himself. He had subdued armed killers without having to draw his gun. He could quiet a fighting drunk by looking at him.

Yet for the first time in almost twenty years, he was wondering. Wondering if he could handle the trouble that would come when the results of the new survey were known. Sam Farley understood the undying hatred that lived in the hearts of some of the country's inhabitants. He knew how they were going to take the news that a ten-mile strip of their richest grazing land was going back to the Cheyenne.

He reached Doc Williams' gate and went through. He walked to the door, knocked and stepped inside.

Mart lay on Doc's couch, his pants down around his knees. Doc was working on his leg.

The air was strong with the smell of sweat and horse manure.

Sam Farley grinned. 'Looks like when a man got into a fight he'd pick a better place for it than a pile of horse manure. Couldn't find a pig pen anyplace?'

Doc Williams said testily, 'Shut up, Sam. Let him alone until I stop hurtin' him.'

'Bullet wound?'

'Pitchfork.'

'Who did it?'

'He didn't say.' Doc turned his head and looked at Mart's face. It was white and the eyes were closed. He said, 'You'll have to ask him later, when he comes to. He's out cold.'

Sam said, 'Looks like he took a pretty good beating too.'

Doc grunted. 'If Mart looks like this, I'd like to see the other guy.'

Sam Farley sat down in a rocker and began to rock idly. Doc finished opening and cleaning the pitchfork wound, then bandaged it up. He got a pan of water and began to wash Mart's face. When he had finished, he dried it, then cleaned out the cuts and abrasions with alcohol. The sting brought back Mart's consciousness, and he opened his eyes.

Turning his head, he saw Farley sitting in the chair. 'Hello Sam.'

'You look kind of peaked, son. Who you been fightin' with?'

'Max.'

'What about?'

'Later.'

Doc snorted angrily. 'You'd think I was a gossipy old woman, the way he acts. Well to hell with both of you. Keep your goddam little secrets if that's the way you feel!'

Sam said calmly, 'What was it all about, Mart?'

'Marian. Max went over there last night and beat her up.'

'Why, for God's sake?'

'Said she was half Indian. Because her ma was taken by the Cheyenne.'

'Where were Ben and Ed?'

'Gone someplace when it happened, I guess. Both of them wanted to go kill the son-of-a-bitch as soon as they found out about it, but Marian wouldn't let 'em.'

'So they came after you. Did they want to sign a complaint?'

'Not after I got out there they didn't.'

'So you took it on yourself to beat him up. Is that it?'

'Uh huh. And if you want to fire me over it why you just go ahead and fire me.'

'Don't tell me what to do. Maybe I'll fire you and maybe I won't, but I'll decide. What's Max look like?'

Mart shrugged, and winced when he did. 'He was out cold when I left. In the middle of the horse corral.' He sat up on the couch and pulled his pants up. He stood up to finish, his

36

face whitening as he did. He buckled his belt, then reached for his cartridge belt and holstered gun.

Doc said, 'Stay off that leg as much as you can. Let me see it again tomorrow.'

Sam said, 'Bill the county for this, Doc. Come on, Mart.'

He held the door for his deputy and followed him outside. Mart limped painfully to the gate, untied his horse and led him down the street toward the jail. Sam kept pace with him.

Mart said thoughtfully, 'You'd think after twenty years some of that hate would cool.'

'Cool hell! When they find out about this new survey . . .'

Mart was silent. They reached the jail. Mart tied his horse and followed Sam inside. He went over and sank down on the leather-covered couch, keeping his leg straight as he did. He stared at the floor several moments, then lifted his glance to Farley. 'What about Mrs. Colfax, Sam? Was she . . . ?'

'Make a difference does it?'

'Not to me it don't.'

'You sure?'

'Sure I'm sure. I'll give Marian time to get over this. Then I'm going courting again.'

'Then why do you want to know?'

A faint touch of color came to Mart's face. He did not reply.

Sam Farley stared at him thoughtfully. 'You

37

know how the plains tribes were with a woman. She was the common property of every buck in the war party until they got back to their village. If she was still alive when they did, she belonged to the one that actually captured her. Sometimes he made her one of his wives. Sometimes she was just a slave for his other wives.'

Mart did not look up. Sam said, 'Sarah Colfax wasn't no exception. But that doesn't prove one of them bucks sired Marian. Sarah was taken in December. Marian was born in August. It could have been either way.'

'Then nobody's ever going to know.'

Sam Farley's glance was steady. 'Nobody's got to know. I know Marian Colfax and so do you. We both know all we need to know about her.' He watched Mart carefully after that. If Mart protested, if he defended himself, it would mean Marian's origin did matter to him.

But Mart didn't raise his head. He didn't speak. Farley released a long, slow sigh, and his mouth made the faintest of smiles.

He looked up as a buckboard came to a halt out front. He stared at the two occupants. He murmured softly, 'Here's your friends.'

He walked to the door and went outside. He could hear Mart coming along behind. He stared up at Otto Gleason, on the buckboard seat, and at Max beside him.

Max looked even worse than Mart did, he decided. Both his eyes were swelling shut, and there was a blue welt almost as big as a walnut on one cheekbone from a ruptured vein. His mouth was swelled and puffy. He was scowling murderously.

Otto glared down at Farley. 'You fire that deputy, Sam. You fire him or . . .'

Farley's voice was very soft. 'Or what, Otto?'

'Or by God you lose my vote at the next election. You lose every vote out at my place.'

'You tell your men how to vote?'

Otto's face reddened. 'They vote the way I do.'

'You approve of beatin' women up?'

'We ain't talkin' about women. We're talkin' about an Injun squaw.'

Farley felt a sudden rush of anger. He said deliberately, 'Who's going to fight Max's battles when you're gone, Otto?'

Max said thickly, 'God damn it, pa, I told you . . .'

'Shut up, Max.' Otto stared furiously at the sheriff. He said, 'Twenty years ago me and my boy came home off roundup. We found the place burned and the bodies of my woman and two little girls layin' out front. I hate them goddam redskins, Farley. I hate them redskins wors'n the Lord hates sin. An' to find out one of 'em was fixin' to marry Max . . . Why I'd of had Cheyennes for grandchildren. You hear me, man? Redskins for grandchildren!'

'If they were Marian Colfax's kids, I'd say you did pretty good.'

'You goin' to fire that deputy?'

'No.'

For an instant there was utter silence. The two old men stared at each other implacably. A war began here in the quiet street of Medicine Lodge between these two ancient giants. The first battle was fought in silence and ended indecisively in a draw.

Without speaking again, Otto Gleason slapped the backs of his team with the reins and the buckboard whirled away down the street.

Sam Farley frowned. This was the first battle over Marian Colfax's heritage. The next battle would come when Otto Gleason learned of the new survey.

Otto Gleason, for all his useless legs, his immobility, would be the leader of the white settlers. He and his son were the ones with the strongest hate. Farley wondered how the news would come. Notices to vacate, he supposed, from the Indian Bureau in Washington. He permitted himself a sour grin as he pictured Otto Gleason reading his notice, reading it for the first time out of a clear blue sky. The grin widened. If Otto didn't die of heart failure, it would be a miracle.

But it wasn't funny. It wasn't funny at all. Because none of the people affected was the kind to fight things out in the courts. They'd been fighting their own battles so long they didn't know any other way.

40

They'd refuse to vacate. They'd probably carry out night raids on the Indian villages inside the reservation. And the Cheyennes would retaliate.

He felt cold inside himself at the thought. An Indian uprising wasn't unthinkable. Only four years ago Custer had been wiped out at the Little Big Horn.

Behind him, Mart Leathers said, 'Thanks, Sam. Thanks for backing me.'

Sam Farley turned his head. His grin was gone, and his eyes were sober. Almost angrily he said, 'Why can't they forget? The Indians that killed his wife and kids are probably all dead by now. When they do get notices to vacate that strip of land ... Hell those notices will just be an excuse—the excuse they've been waiting for all these years. An excuse to start things up all over again.'

'How long do you think it'll be?'

Farley frowned. 'The surveyors have been gone almost a month. It could come any time.'

Mart asked, 'You need me for the rest of the day? I could sure use a little sleep.'

'Go ahead.' Farley waited until Mart started up the street. He called, 'Do me a favor, will you?'

Mart stopped, waited without turning.

Farley said, 'Take a bath.'

Mart muttered something that Farley didn't hear. Then he went on up the street.

The sheriff went inside the jail and sat down

41

in the swivel chair. He put his feet up on the desk, noticing the scars made by his spurs in the years that were past and gone.

A lot of memories went into those twenty years. Like the look on Sarah Colfax's face when she saw him among the troopers that had rescued her. Like the sight of a body swinging gently in the breeze beneath the gnarled old limb of a cottonwood. Like the look in a killer's eyes the instant before he reaches for his gun.

Farley had never been married, but he'd almost been. Another girl had been taken by the same raiding party that had taken Sarah Colfax. Only that girl hadn't survived the ordeal. She was dead when the war party reached the village several days following the raid.

So Sam Farley had his own reasons to hate the Cheyennes. Yet with Sam, the years had dulled his hate. He knew he couldn't revenge himself against the whole Cheyenne nation for the acts of half a dozen men.

Thoughtfully, he pulled a pipe and a pouch of tobacco from his pocket. He packed the pipe and lighted it.

He felt, suddenly, like a man in the path of an avalanche. He could see it coming and knew it would engulf him. Yet he also knew he could not escape. All he could do was wait.

CHAPTER FIVE

Ben Colfax was not, normally, a devious man. Big and blocky and loose-moving, he faced the problems that arose in his life in a direct and uncomplicated way.

Yet this problem was different than the others had been. Last night he would have gone to Gleasons', called Max out, and shot it out with him—if Marian hadn't stopped him.

But she had stopped him. And Max Gleason had gotten away with manhandling her.

All day he rode the wide reaches of the ranch and the strip of grazing land north of it, the strip that separated the reservation from the Colfax ranch and those of Gleason and Heller. Time did not cool his anger, nor did it diminish his determination that, one way or another, Max would pay for what he had done to Marian.

The one burning question in his mind was how. How could he make Gleason pay?

The sun sank toward the low, rolling country in the direction of Medicine Lodge. He turned and started back toward home.

Something caught his eye . . . He turned his horse slightly toward it.

Staring down, he saw that it was a Cheyenne arrow. Its point was buried in the ground. The feathered shaft stuck up at an angle.

Fired at a deer or antelope, he supposed, it had missed. Perhaps the brave who had fired it had gone on in pursuit of his game. Or perhaps he hadn't been able to find the arrow when he looked for it.

But it gave Ben Colfax an idea. He got down from his horse and pulled the arrow out of the ground. He stared at it thoughtfully.

The point was iron, one of those shipped from the east by the thousands and sold to the Indians who valued them because they were sharper than stone and less trouble to use.

He swung to the back of his horse, the arrow in his hand. His face took on a look of grim satisfaction. He had been heading straight toward home, but now he turned suddenly and headed for the Gleason place. There *was* a way. This Cheyenne arrow had given him the idea.

Previously he had ridden rather aimlessly, taking his time. Now he rode in a direct line, spurring the horse into a steady, rolling lope. He crossed the line onto Gleason's place as the sun dropped its blazing rim below the horizon far beyond the town.

And he began to scan the land carefully. He began to watch the ground.

The sun put a blazing afterglow on a few high, scattered clouds. Ben picked up a trail and turned into it, still traveling fast. He rode along the plain, fresh trail for about a mile and a half before he suddenly pulled his horse up

44

and reached for the rifle in the saddle boot.

The sky was wholly gray by now. He dismounted, sighted carefully, and fired once. With a look of satisfaction on his face, he shoved the rifle back into the boot without ejecting the empty cartridge and mounted again. He scanned the surrounding countryside as he rode, but saw nothing against the lighter area of sky above the rapidly darkening land.

He reached the animal he had shot and dismounted beside it, still holding the arrow in his hand. He looked at the brand first, satisfying himself that it was Gleason's brand. Then he looked for the wound and found it almost immediately, just behind the animal's shoulder.

Carefully he inserted the arrow point into the wound. Carefully, holding the arrow shaft firmly in both his hands, he shoved it deep into the still-warm carcass of the steer.

Hands on hips, he stared down at his work for several moments. Then he rose, mounted his horse, and headed toward home without looking back.

He had hurt them by killing one of their steers, of course. But there was a lot more to it than that. Knowing the hatred both Otto and Max felt for the Cheyennes ... He began to smile grimly to himself.

Neither Otto nor Max would be able to take a thing like this. Nor would they go to the law.

The law was too cumbersome, and, besides, civilian lawmen had no jurisdiction over the Cheyennes. No, the Gleasons would take their revenge for the murdered steer in a much more direct way. They'd take their revenge directly against the Cheyennes.

The Indians would take it from there. Or maybe the U.S. Government would. All Ben had to do was go home and wait.

*   *   *

Mart Leathers lived in a tiny, one-room house at the edge of town. It sat back on its lot from the street, the way Doc Williams' house did. It had a small stable out in back where Mart kept his horse.

On the morning following the fight, he awoke at six, as he usually did, and for a moment laid still in bed staring at the sunlight streaming through the open window. His face felt puffy and strange. He knew that when he moved he'd find every muscle stiff and sore as hell.

When he did move, it was suddenly, and his face twisted with the pain. In his underwear and bare feet, he limped outside, pumped a bucket of water, and carried it inside. He built a fire in the stove and put the water on to heat.

Waiting, he rolled himself a cigarette and smoked it, staring at the stove. Maybe it was too soon, but he'd waited a long, long time. He was going out to see Marian today.

The stove began to roar softly. The water heated. Mart got down the tub and poured the water into it. He went outside again and pumped another bucket of cold water from the pump. He dumped that into the tub too. Then he stripped off his underwear and got uncomfortably into the tub, letting his feet hang out, trying to keep the leg bandage dry.

He bathed, got out and dried, and found clean clothes to put on. He shaved, made coffee, and drank two cups. Then he buckled on his gun and belt and went out to the stable behind the house. He saddled his horse, mounted stiffly, and rode toward the center of town.

Medicine Lodge was one of the first towns in the territory. Its main street had been unchanged for almost fifteen years. It was lined on both sides by frame, false-fronted buildings. At the upper end, there was a great, yellow, two-story hotel, a mercantile store, a dressmaker's shop, six saloons, and a saddlemaker's shop. Farther down, near the railroad station, there was a gunsmith's shop, two livery barns, and two parlor houses, their shades drawn down this morning against the early sun.

A mangy looking mongrel dog was scratching himself in the middle of the street. He looked up and wagged his tail tentatively as Mart Leathers passed. A man came out of

Flora's, turned and cursed someone inside, then walked unsteadily up the street.

Mart reached the jail, a small, square stone building, and dismounted in front of it. He looped his horse's reins around the rail and limped inside.

Sam Farley sat at his desk in the swivel chair, his spurred boots on the desk. He looked at Mart. 'You look like you might make it after all. How's the leg?'

Mart grinned. 'Stiffer'n hell.' He stared at Farley for several moments. 'I hate to keep askin' for time off, but I'd like to ride out and see Marian today.'

Farley shrugged. 'Go ahead. Nothin' much to do anyway. But go down to the post office and get the mail first.'

Mart nodded. He hesitated a moment, then turned and went outside again.

The post office adjoined the railroad station. He rode down there, tied his horse, and went inside. Leonard Peevey, the elderly postmaster, was sorting mail. Mart stood at the barred window and asked, 'Anything for Sam or me?'

Peevey turned his head. He wore a pair of gold-rimmed glasses pinched to his nose. From them dangled a black cord, which was secured to one of the buttons of his vest. He wore a green eyeshade and black sleeve protectors that were gathered with elastic just above his elbows. He handed Mart several envelopes, holding several others in his other hand.

Mart couldn't help glancing at them because they were larger, different from the rest of the mail. In the upper left-hand corner he could see the words, 'Indian Bureau' and 'Washington, D.C.' He said, 'Let me take a look at one of those.'

'It's addressed to Otto Gleason.'

'Let me see it anyway.'

Peevey handed him the envelope doubtfully. Mart stared down at it. Lifting his glance, he asked, 'Who else got one of these?'

'Ben Colfax. Heller. Duer.'

Mart handed back the envelope. He said, 'Thanks,' turned, and left the post office. He untied his horse, mounted, and rode back to the jail.

He went in and gave the mail to Farley. He said, 'The notices you were expecting are down at the post office. From the Indian Bureau. One's going to Otto Gleason. Others are going to Ben Colfax and Heller and Joe Duer.'

Farley nodded. He showed no visible emotion, but his jaw was clamped tight. Mart went out, swung to the back of his horse and rode out toward the east, toward the Colfax place thirteen miles from town. Hell, hate or no hate, the ranchers using that strip of reservation land would just have to give it up. They had no choice. They couldn't fight the whole Northern Cheyenne nation. Neither could they fight the U.S. Army, which would be given the job of enforcing the edict if it was not obeyed. They might not like giving up that ten-mile strip of rich grazing land, but there wasn't much else that they could do.

He put the matter out of his mind, then, and thought about Marian Colfax. He began to feel tremors in his knees at the thought of seeing her again.

Maybe she wouldn't even see him, he thought. Maybe she was still too shaken up by her experience. Or maybe she just plain didn't want to see him.

Once or twice during the long ride, he almost turned and went back. But each time he continued, his jaw firming determinedly. Maybe it was too soon. And maybe she didn't ever want to see him again. But she'd have to tell him that herself.

She was in the yard hanging out clothes when he arrived. Ben was not around, but Ed was working in the blacksmith shop shoeing a horse. Mart rode to where Marian was and looked down at her. There was still evidence of Gleason's fists on her face. One of her eyes was almost black, and her mouth seemed puffy. He said, 'Hello, Marian.'

She did not quite meet his eyes. 'Hello Mart.'

'I . . .' He cleared his throat. 'You mind if I get off this horse?'

'No. I don't mind. Why should I mind?'

He swung off the horse. Trying not to limp,

he went over to the corral and tied the animal. Then he came back. Marian said, 'You look like you'd been in a fight.'

'Uh huh.' He hoped she'd drop the subject because he was going to feel like a fool if she asked who he'd been fighting with.

She asked, 'Who with?' She had clothespins in her mouth, and she did not look at him.

'Max.'

She looked up, startled. 'Because of me?'

He felt his face grow hot. Defensively he said, 'Well, you wouldn't let Ben and Ed do anything. And you didn't want to swear out a complaint. I was damned ... darned if he was going to get away with doing what he did.'

She was silent for a long, long time. She finished hanging out the clothes in the basket on the ground and picked it up. Then she asked, 'You want some coffee, Mart?'

'Sure. That'd be fine.'

'Then come on inside.'

He took the empty basket from her and followed her into the house. He put the basket down and stood in the doorway uncomfortably.

Marian said, 'Sit down Mart.'

He sat down at the oilcloth-covered kitchen table. He watched her move around. She was fresh, and clean, and slim. She made a kind of hunger stir in him.

Once she turned and looked straight into his eyes. She said simply, 'Thank you Mart.'

51

He cleared his throat uneasily. 'I'd like to come see you sometimes, Marian.'

She was silent for a long time after that, her face turned away from him. When she finally turned, there was an unaccustomed bitterness in the set of her mouth, and there was a suspicion of tears in her eyes. 'Why, Mart? Do you want a Cheyenne squaw for a wife?'

He said, angrily, 'You just stop that kind of talk right now! Any damn fool can tell just by looking at you . . .'

'Max couldn't.'

He snorted disgustedly. 'Him!'

She turned and came toward him, coffee pot in one hand, a cup in the other. He said, 'Anyhow, it don't matter to me. If a man went around asking for pedigrees from every girl . . .' He grinned up at her. 'Well hell, don't you see what I'm getting at? A man's a fool if he can't believe in his own feelings about someone.'

She put a cup in front of him and poured it full. There was a fresh woman fragrance about her that stirred the elusive hunger in him again.

He said, 'I'd still like to come see you sometimes.'

'All right, Mart.' Her voice was scarcely audible. She got herself a cup of coffee and sat down across from him. The bitterness was gone from her mouth, but her eyes still held the suspicion of brightness they had shown before.

He found himself wondering suddenly what Ben and Ed, her brothers, would do when they got the notices from the Indian Bureau. They also had cause for hating the Cheyennes. Would they take it better than Otto and Max Gleason, or would they, too, take the law into their own hands?

And if they did, what would he do? He'd have to go against Marian's brothers or resign his job. If he resigned he'd be condoning something he knew was wrong.

It was possible, of course, that the situation would not result in violence. But he didn't believe it. He knew better. He knew that in a day or two, when all of those receiving them had read the notices to vacate their grazing land, all hell was going to break loose hereabouts. And he'd be caught right in the middle of it.

CHAPTER SIX

Mart Leathers did not hate the Cheyenne like most of those in the country south of the reservation did, perhaps because he understood them better than anyone else.

Riding back toward town from the Colfax place, he felt a warm excitement as he thought of seeing Marian again. But he also felt the coldness of dread, dread of the conflict he knew was sure to come.

Mart had been five at the time of the atrocities that had so embittered the settlers of Pawnee County. But he had not been here. He had been several hundred miles south of here, in the land that was Colorado Territory now. And his experience had been quite different from the experiences suffered by the people here.

He and his mother and father lived in a small house built of sod, roofed with poles and boards salvaged from their wagon, and sunk into the ground of a shallow hillside to give it warmth in winter, coolness in summer.

But it was damp as well. And the winter he was five, both his father and mother took sick.

He didn't know what the sickness was. He vaguely remembered their flushed faces, the heat of their bodies, the lethargy into which both of them sank. And one frosty morning he awoke to find that the bodies of both were cold.

At five, he had not really understood death. He had only been hungry, and cold. He had built up the fire, and had eaten what he could find. He had probably supposed they would eventually awake, he thought now, but they had not awakened. Instead, after a few days, they had begun to smell until he could no longer stand it inside the house. So he'd started out, walking, intending to find help for them.

How far he walked, or for how long, he had no idea. A few miles at most, he supposed. And then he had encountered a hunting party of Cheyenne braves.

He ran in fear from them, and they dismounted to pursue on foot. He ran like a rabbit and succeeded in eluding them for quite a while. But in the end one of them caught up with him.

And then he fought. Like a small wildcat. He kicked and clawed and bit but it did no good. The Cheyenne only laughed delightedly at him, and said guttural words of approval in the Cheyenne tongue.

They took him back to their village and fed him and let him sleep in warm robes inside a leather tepee that smelled of smoke, and food, and human occupancy. When he awoke, he was fed again, and dressed in clothing like the Cheyenne children wore.

He had a new father and mother, dark-skinned ones who had lost their own son by drowning the spring before. And he was raised as though he were one of the Cheyennes himself.

His skin grew dark from constant exposure to the sun. He played with the other Indian children, and his education was their education, at the feet of his foster father, or at the feet of the old ones whose years had given them wisdom.

He forgot English and learned to speak the Cheyenne tongue. And he learned something else few white men ever learn. He learned that there was much good in the Indian way of life. He learned their gentleness, their undeviating honesty, their respect and love for others of their kind. And he learned love for this open prairie land, which had been their home almost from time immemorial.

Nor were all the atrocities committed by Indians. When Mart was ten, the village in which he lived was attacked by a troop of U.S. Army cavalry.

Many of the people were killed. The village itself was burned. Mart was among those captured and the clothing he had been wearing when the Cheyennes found him was discovered in one of the lodges before it was burned.

A new life began for Mart, as unfamiliar and unwanted as this one had been at first. He was taken to Fort Laramie on the Platte. He was taken into the house of one of the sergeant's wives.

He ran away, and, riding a stolen horse, went in search of his Indian friends. Lost in a blizzard, he stumbled onto a sod shanty similar to the one in which he had been raised.

Here he stayed until he was grown, until the man and woman who had taken him in and loved him as their own gave up their attempt at homesteading and returned to the East where they had come from originally. They wanted Mart to go with them, but he could not bear to leave this land where he had been raised.

He carried their name, Leathers. His given name, Martin, was the name they gave him when he was ten. What his original name had been he had no idea.

But he knew one thing, certainly. He was alive because of the Cheyennes. Without them, he would have died of starvation and cold, on the endless, empty plain. He owed them more than that, though. For accepting him, for teaching him things about them that few white men ever learn.

He knew something else, as certainly. Understanding both sides of the coming conflict would not make his existence any easier. Ultimately, he would have to take a stand, for one side or the other. He could not stay on the fence.

His face worried, he spurred his horse toward town.

*   *   *

He arrived a little after noon. The pitchfork wound in his leg ached steadily. The town drowsed at noonday. The street was virtually empty. He rode directly to the jail and swung down from his horse.

He limped to the bench at one side of the

door and sank down beside the sheriff, who was sitting there with his legs stretched out, his hat tilted forward to shield his eyes from the glare in the street.

Farley asked, 'See her? Is she all right?'

Mart nodded. 'She seems all right. Her face is marked up some. If I'd seen her face before I went over to Gleason's yesterday I'd probably have killed the son-of-a-bitch.'

Farley didn't reply. There was something in his face . . . Mart asked suddenly, 'Did all of them come in and get their mail?'

'One of Gleason's men was in. Clem Heller got his. And Ed Colfax was in.'

'So now we wait. Isn't there something we can do?'

'Not a thing. Not until somebody else does something. So far nobody has broken any laws. Maybe they'll just refuse to vacate the strip. If they do that, then it'll be up to the Army to move them out.'

'What if the Indians move into it?'

Sam Farley shrugged.

'Would it do any good if I went out and talked to them? To the Cheyennes, I mean.'

'Might. They'll listen to you a damn sight quicker'n they will any one else.'

'I'll do it, then. I'll get something to eat and a fresh horse.'

He sat there a moment more, briefly enjoying his own motionlessness, dreading the long ride to the reservation. His leg would be killing him by the time he got back. He got up reluctantly.

He led his horse to Mike Androvich's restaurant, half a block up the street, and tied him out in front. He went around the building to the rear, worked the pump handle until a stream of water gushed from it. He washed his hands, splashed some water into his face, then dried both his face and hands on a soiled towel hanging beside the pump. He went in by the back door, through the kitchen, and sat down at the counter out in front.

Mike was fat, bald, and dark, and his skin gleamed with sweat. He swiped the counter in front of Mart with a damp rag and grinned, showing two gold teeth in front. 'You look like you tangled with a buzz saw.'

Mart grunted sourly. He wondered if he was going to have to explain to everyone he saw. He said, 'Give me some of whatever you're cooking.'

'Roast beef. Thirty cents.'

Mart nodded. He fished makings from his pocket and rolled a cigarette. He lighted it and smoked idly while he waited. He doubted if the Cheyennes were going to be very helpful when he talked to them. They needed that ten-mile strip as badly as the ranchers did. They needed the game that was on it. Their own lands were pretty well hunted out.

They'd been hunting it on the sly for years, of course. But always cautiously, and only when their need was desperate.

Mike Androvich brought him his dinner, and he ate hungrily. Finished, he laid thirty cents on the counter, rose, and went out. He mounted his horse and rode to the livery stable where he hired another. Leading his own horse, he rode back home and put the animal in the stable out behind the house. He pumped water for him and threw him some hay. He went out again, mounted, and rode out of town, heading north.

Now that he was embarked on this, he wondered how much good, if any, it was going to do. He didn't know any of the Cheyennes. He had probably forgotten much of their language.

They had no reason to trust him. Particularly when he asked them to stay off of land that rightfully was theirs. To them it would no doubt seem like another white man's trick.

Numbers, of course, were on the Indians' side. They outnumbered the Gleasons, Colfaxes, Hellers, and Duers, and their crews by fifty to a hundred to one. They could take the strip of land and hold it no matter what the ranchers did or tried to do.

The danger, the real danger lay in the animosity felt by the whites in this area toward the Cheyenne. And in the tendency of the government to back the whites in every dispute that came up. If the Cheyennes were hotheaded or if they could be goaded into rashness . . . If the Army had to come into the dispute and put down an uprising . . . then the Indians would lose the land the new survey had given them.

Otto Gleason would be aware of this possibility. So would Ben Colfax. So would Clem Heller and Joe Duer.

All the ranchers had to do was anger the Cheyennes—anger them enough to make them retaliate.

Mart pushed his horse hard. The reservation boundary lay north of Medicine Lodge by thirty miles. The village nearest the boundary was another five.

The hours passed slowly. Mart alternately galloped his horse and let him trot. The combination of gaits ate the miles without unduly tiring the horse. The sun sank slowly across the western sky.

It hung like an orange ball just over the horizon when Mart brought the Indian village into view.

It rested in a small valley through which a narrow stream ran. It did not look like the Cheyenne villages Mart remembered. Only a few of the tepees were of buffalo hide. Others were made of canvas obtained from the whites, or cowhide. There were a couple of small log cabins, and half a dozen shacks thrown up from scrap lumber and sheet iron.

A couple of dozen dogs rushed from the

village as he approached, and ran at his horse's heels, snarling, snapping, sometimes fighting among themselves.

A number of curious Indians gathered at the village edge to watch him as he approached. Their dress was not as he remembered it. It showed a carelessness he had never noticed in the Cheyennes before. Some of the squaws were dirty, their hair uncombed.

Nor were their expressions proud and serene as he remembered them. They were sullen and hostile. Like the face of a dog that would like to growl but fears the consequences.

Mart halted his horse before them. He gave the universal sign of peace and friendship. He said, haltingly, in Cheyenne, 'I have words for your chief and medicine men. Tell them I am here.'

A boy of about fifteen turned and disappeared among the lodges of the village. Mart sat his horse in silence, waiting. The Indians stared up impassively at him.

Mart felt suddenly depressed and sad. The Cheyennes had come a long way from those he remembered as a boy. These were beaten people. Their pride was gone. They had learned fear of the whites, but they had not learned trust.

And why should they trust, Mart thought bitterly. They had been cheated in every dealing they ever had with the whites. They knew they would be cheated again. They could not even count on retaining this reservation, this land the whites had given them forever. They knew they could only hold it so long as the whites thought it valueless.

He saw a group of men come from the direction the boy had gone. He waited until they reached him and then he said, 'I would talk.'

A tall old man, standing in front of the others said, 'We have nothing to talk about.'

'I am your friend. I was raised in the Southern Cheyenne village of Bear Claw. I am the adopted son of Slow Knife.'

'You are a white. You wear the star of the white man's law.'

'Hear me.'

The old one turned and looked questioningly at the three behind him. One of them nodded slightly. He turned his head and looked at Mart. 'Come with me.'

Mart followed them as they walked back into the village. They halted before one of the buffalo hide tepees, and he dismounted. He followed them inside.

To him, it was almost like coming home. The smells, the sight of the fire in the center, the beds of robes on the far side, the squaws working silently.

He took his place beside the fire and squatted there. He sat in silence while the chief lighted a pipe, pointed the stem at the four points of the compass, at the heavens, and at the earth.

He took the pipe in turn, smoked it briefly, then passed it on. When all had smoked, he said, 'The white men who measure the land have said that some of the white man's land belongs to you.'

The chief nodded. 'We know. The Indian Agent has told us that.'

'There are white men using it who do not want to give it up. They will not give it up until they are forced to do so. They will try to trick the Cheyenne out of it.'

All four now looked at Mart suspiciously. At last the old chief said, 'You are of the whites, who hate the Cheyenne. It is our belief that you are trying to trick us now.'

Mart said, ignoring the statement, 'They know how the Father in Washington thinks. They will goad the Cheyennes into violence. When the Cheyennes can stand no more of their goading and decide to fight, then will the pony soldiers of the whites come and fight with the Cheyennes. The Father in Washington will think that the promises of the Cheyenne to live in peace are lies. He will take the land back from the Cheyennes. He may take all the land they have and send them to the south where their brothers are.'

The four stared at him, suspicion and distrust showing in their otherwise expressionless faces. Not one of them spoke.

Mart said, 'Do not be like the fish in the stream and take the bait the white men throw to you. If the white men trespass on your land, go to the Indian Agent and tell him what has been done. Let him punish the men.'

Still none of the four old ones spoke. Mart waited for them to say something for a long, long time. At last he realized they did not intend to speak. He got up and left the lodge. In silence, he mounted his horse and rode back out of the village the way he had come in.

Coming here had been a mistake, as he had feared it might be. They had heard him, but they had not believed. They had mistrusted him and he couldn't blame them for doing so. They would probably never trust any white again.

But when the trouble came ... when Gleason and the others began their needling raids ... perhaps they would remember his coming and the words he had said to them. He could only hope they would.

CHAPTER SEVEN

At sundown, Della Chavez came onto the porch of the Gleason house, pushing a chair that had been equipped with wheels. She positioned it next to Otto Gleason's chair and

65

he hitched himself laboriously into it. She pushed him into the house, into the parlor and beyond, through the huge dining room to the kitchen, which already smelled of cooking meat.

Leaving him, she continued preparation of the meal. Otto fumbled in his pocket, withdrew the notice received today from the Indian Bureau and read it over again. 'You are hereby given notice ... to vacate ... on or before the 7th day of October, 1880 ...'

He stared at it a moment, eyes smoldering. Then, suddenly he methodically tore it into little bits. Della turned to look at him. Silently she got broom and dustpan and swept up the pieces from the floor at his feet.

He said bitterly, 'The dirty bastards! They sit on their butts in some office in Washington and tell me to get off that land. And as if that wasn't enough, they give me five days to do it in!'

He heard the sound of a fast galloping horse outside the house. He heard one of the hands yell, 'Max! Hey Max!'

After that, he heard nothing for quite a while. His eyes continued to burn and his mouth was a thin, straight line. Damn it, if he only had the use of his legs!

Max came into the house. He was carrying a Cheyenne arrow with blood in the point and a third of the way up the shaft. He said furiously, 'You know what this came out of? One of our steers. Not five miles from here!'

Otto felt a rush of fury, sudden fury that came as quickly as Max's unexpected words had come. This was what you got when you treated the damned redskins like human beings. Give them a reservation and the first thing you knew they wanted more. They should've been exterminated in the first place. If Otto had his way . . .

He stared at his son. He could ride on a buggy seat, but he couldn't ride a horse. Whatever was done would have to be done by Max. But Max had been nine at the time Cheyennes killed his mother and sisters and burned the house. He had seen the bodies. He hated Cheyennes too.

There was something, though . . . Otto stared more closely at Max's face. Max met his eyes as long as he could, then looked uneasily away.

Max's eyes were both black, and one of them had been swelled shut yesterday. He'd lost a front tooth. His mouth was puffy and in places dark with dried blood.

Otto scowled. What was it that bothered him about Max? Max had been running the ranch all right. He'd put up a good enough fight with the deputy, even though he'd lost. He said, 'You and the hands saddle up right after supper. If you ride hard, you can hit one of their villages about midnight. Take along some cans of coal oil.'

Max had his back to his father. He was getting a cup of coffee from the stove. The arrow lay on the table, within reach of Otto's hand. He picked it up, almost the way a man who hates snakes will pick up a dead one. Gingerly. Not as though he feared it but as though it was repulsive to him.

An arrow had been in his wife's body when he found her that day so long ago—broken off by the Indians after she was dead, but there, buried in her soft, white flesh ... He felt a sudden touch of nausea in his stomach and a lightness in his head. Max might hate, but his hatred could not be compared to that of his father.

Max turned around, a cup of coffee in his hand. Some of it spilled and dripped onto the floor. Otto stared at him unbelievingly.

The anger was gone from Max's eyes, along with it the outrage at the arrow having been found in a Gleason steer. His face had lost some of its color. He would not meet his father's eyes.

Otto said harshly, 'Max!'

Max glanced at him and glanced away. Otto said implacably, 'Didn't you hear what I said?'

'I heard.'

'Then why the hell don't you say something? Why won't you look at me?'

Max turned his head and met his father's eyes determinedly. Otto stared in unbelief. He said, 'Why you yellow pup, you're scared!'

68

The words brought a flush to Max's face but no words to his lips.

Otto glared furiously for a moment, then shouted angrily, 'Maybe you don't remember the things I do! Maybe you don't remember the naked, bloody bodies of your mother and two sisters laying right out there in the yard on the bloody ground. You got any idea what was done to your mother? You got any idea of the knife work them dirty redskins done? Or wasn't you close enough to see? Well I'll tell you, boy. They . . .'

Max shouted, 'Stop it! Damn you, pa, stop it!'

'Don't you curse me! And don't you yell at me! If I want you to listen, by God you'll listen! Them stinkin' Injuns . . .'

Max whirled suddenly. He rushed from the kitchen. The door slammed and for an instant there was utter silence in the room. Then Otto heard the sound of Max vomiting outside in the yard.

He felt sick at his stomach himself. Sick with disgust at his son's fear. Then his old eyes turned hard. Fear or no fear, Max would do what had to be done. Otto would force him if he had to. The only way to keep that ten-mile strip of land was to torment the Indians until they retaliated and the government intervened.

*　　　*　　　*

69

Outside in the yard, Max vomited until he could bring up no more. Even then he dry-heaved until his stomach felt like it had been kicked by a mule.

Weak and sweating, he staggered across the yard to the pump. He leaned on it for a long, long time, breathing harshly and shallowly. Then he worked the pump-handle and stuck his face under the spout.

He gulped water, straightened, and spit the last mouthful out. He stared in the direction of the house.

He wished his mind could stop seeing that blackened pile of smoldering timbers where the old house had been. He wished it could stop seeing the red and white naked bodies lying scattered like broken dolls. Seeing his mother and sisters that way had been an obscenity that he knew he would not get over until he died.

What kind of animals could do that to another human being, he wondered now. What kind of depraved mentality could squat beside a naked body working on it with a knife? He shuddered and felt his stomach cramp again.

He bent double, hugging it. His sweaty body began to chill.

But the chill was not altogether caused by his drying sweat. Part of it was caused by fear. There was a singular difference between Max

70

and his father. Both of them hated Cheyennes. Both of them hated with equal intensity, but Max was also afraid of them. His father was not.

He began to shake violently. He gripped his hands into fists furiously, trying to stop their trembling. His father wanted him to ride to the reservation tonight and fire one of their villages. He'd have to go or . . .

In his mind, he faced the unpalatable alternative. His father wouldn't tolerate cowardice in his son. Unless he went tonight, he had just as well leave the ranch. There would be no appeasing his father's bitter hatred of the Cheyennes. It was burn the Cheyenne village or leave here, never to return.

He considered what it would be like to leave. He'd never been anyplace but Medicine Lodge. He'd never been out of Pawnee County in his life.

Not only that. If he left, his father would disinherit him. He'd lose this ranch. He'd lose the place that was home to him, that would always be home to him.

However you figured it, it all came back to one thing. He'd have been robbed of the ranch by the Cheyennes. They'd have beaten him. But if he went tonight, if he did what his father had told him to . . . well hell, maybe it wouldn't be so bad. The Indians were different these days. They hadn't made a raid for fifteen years.

They hadn't killed a white in all that time.

He'd have half a dozen men with him. The Indians would be asleep. They could be into the village and out again before any resistance developed. Chances were, the Indians didn't even have guards out at night anymore.

He walked to the bunkhouse. A couple of lamps were burning inside. Usually there was a card game going, sometimes whist, sometimes poker, but the men weren't playing cards tonight. They were gathered around the table, talking. The talk was of the dead steer, of the Cheyennes, of the notice to vacate that Otto had received today.

Max said, 'Saddle up, all of you. Get coal oil and matches and gunny sacks filled with straw. We're going to burn us a village.'

The men trooped past him into the night. He heard a couple of them whoop with excitement. He turned and went back to the house.

Otto still sat in his wheelchair beside the table. Max said, 'All right, pa. We'll go.'

His father looked at him approvingly. The old man knew he was afraid, he thought. The old man also knew how much harder it was to do something when you're afraid.

Right now he didn't seem to care whether his father approved of him or not. He was scared. He was so damned scared his body was cold. If he didn't get started, if he didn't commit himself beyond any possibility of

72

backing out, he might not go through with it at all.

He turned and stalked from the kitchen. He crossed the yard to the corral, where the men were noisily saddling up.

He caught himself a horse and saddled him. By the time he had finished, the men were ready and waiting. Each of them carried a gunnysack filled with straw. Several had coal oil cans. All were armed, both with rifles and revolvers.

Max led out, heading north, but angling slightly west. He knew the location of one village close to the reservation line. It was on the bank of Horsetooth Creek and was located there permanently. The Cheyennes had even built two or three small log cabins.

For a while, the men shouted back and forth at each other. Then, as the hours ate the miles, they fell silent. There were six of them. Max made seven.

Jack Lane was the oldest. He'd gone to work for Otto more than fifteen years ago. Lane was about sixty, grizzled and bearded with a skinny body that looked as if the plains air and sun dried it out.

There was Joe Taplow, and Will Brown, and Luke Zimmerman. The youngest two were Bob Higgins and Frank Valenti. They were both about Max's age.

At the reservation boundary, Max pulled his sweating horse to a halt. He judged it was about midnight. He said, 'We're going to hit the camp on Horsetooth Creek. We'll stop just outside the village and soak the straw with coal oil. As we ride in, light the bags and throw them against the lodges. We'll ride on out, and we ought to be gone before any of them wake up.'

No one said anything. Max said, 'This is the old man's idea. It isn't all revenge for the steer, either. He figures if we can stir the Injuns up enough, they'll fight back. Soon as they do, the Army will move in. The old man figures that when that happens, the government will take that ten-mile strip back from them.'

'They will, too,' Lane said.

'All right then, let's go.'

Now he held his horse to a walk, and when Taplow said something he cautioned angrily, 'Shut up, all of you.'

He reached Horsetooth Creek and followed its winding course north. At last, from a quarter mile, he saw the village ahead of him.

It was completely dark. Not even the remains of a fire glowed. He went on quietly until only about three hundred yards separated him and his men from the clustered tepees and shacks. He said, 'All right. Get down and dump the coal oil over the sacks.'

There was a small stir, the squeaking of saddle leather, the faint clink of coal oil cans. The air was suddenly strong with the smell of coal oil, and he could hear it gurgling out of the cans.

His chest felt as though something were constricting it. He could scarcely breathe. He felt dizzy and lightheaded. More than anything else in the world he wanted to whirl his horse and run.

The men mounted up, leaving the coal oil cans scattered on the ground. The horses were fidgety now, perhaps from the coal oil smell, perhaps from the village smells. Max said, 'Now!'

He spurred his horse straight toward the village, snatching out his gun with his right hand. He thumbed the hammer back.

When only a hundred yards separated them from the sleeping Cheyenne village, Max roared, 'Light 'em!'

Shielding their matches behind the oil-soaked gunnysacks, the men scratched them alight with thumbnails or struck them on the rough butt plates of their rifles. The fire took almost instantly, creeping over the sacks until each was a huge, flaming torch. But they were inside the village now . . .

One by one the flaming bags were flung away, to slam against the sloping hide walls of the tepees. Max and his men thundered through, pursued by frantically barking dogs, by the startled cries of the suddenly awakened Cheyennes.

At the village edge, Max swung around in his saddle and looked back. Five lodges were burning, each sending up a pillar of flame twenty-five feet into the black night air. Figures were running back and forth. A single gunshot sounded, but Max and his men now were in the clear.

In the clear, Max began to shake as though he had a chill. His teeth chattered so loud he thought the men must surely hear. He clenched his jaws tight, until they ached with the pressure he put on them.

But it was done. Now he could go home. And suddenly he was weak with his relief.

Tonight, he did not think that the oil-soaked gunnysacks might have started a fire that would consume the country, perhaps even the entire territory. He did not think of those who might die as a consequence.

He was thinking only of himself. He had done what, earlier, had seemed impossible to him. And now he could go home.

CHAPTER EIGHT

Elvin Burke rode into Medicine Lodge just before noon on the following day. He was a small, wiry man of fifty. Normally amiable, he had a toothy smile and eyes that crinkled at their corners when he smiled. He was not smiling today, and his eyes were hard as bits of stone. Flushed with anger, he dismounted from his lathered horse in front of the sheriff's office.

Sam Farley, sitting on the bench in the sun, stared up at him both curiously and uneasily.

Burke tied his horse, crossed the walk, and glared down at Sam. 'Do you know what happened last night at Angry Bear's village on Horsetooth Creek?'

Farley shook his head.

'A bunch of white men raided it. Burned five lodges and ran. Damn it, Sam, they're asking for trouble, and they'll get all they can handle if they don't watch out. The Cheyennes are mad. No telling what they'll do.'

The door opened and Mart Leathers came outside. He glanced at the Indian Agent and nodded. 'Morning, Mr. Burke.'

Burke nodded shortly at him, his anger unabated. Farley said, 'Burke came in to tell us that someone raided the village on Horsetooth Creek. He says they burned five lodges and ran.'

Burke said tightly, 'What I want to know is what you intend to do about it. If the men responsible aren't caught and punished immediately, I can't answer for what the Cheyennes may do. Good Lord, man, we could have a full-scale uprising if we're not careful. One thing leads to another and the first thing you know . . .'

Farley said, 'Get some horses, Mart. And get a fresh one for Mr. Burke.' He turned his head and glanced at the Agent. 'We'll ride out and see if we can pick up a trail.'

Burke grumbled something unintelligible. Then, slightly mollified, he sat down on the bench beside Farley. He took a cigar from his pocket, bit off the end, and lighted it. His hands trembled as he did.

Mart untied Burke's horse and walked him toward the livery stable. Burke puffed his cigar nervously for several moments. Sam Farley asked, 'Did Angry Bear say he'd wait?'

'I haven't talked to him. I haven't talked to anyone but the runner he sent to the Agency. I told him to tell Angry Bear to wait and not do anything until he heard from me. But hell, Sam, he might not have waited long enough to get the message. He might be on that trail right now.'

He probably was, thought Sam. Furthermore, in taking it, he would be playing into the raiders' hands, doing exactly what they wanted him to do. He said, 'If they start anything, they're likely to find themselves done out of that ten-mile strip the survey gave to them. They could even lose their reservation and be shipped to Oklahoma. Have you told them that?'

'I warned them to be careful a couple of weeks ago,' Burke said irritably. 'But I didn't anticipate anything like this.' He stared at Sam curiously. 'Got any ideas who might have been responsible for that raid?'

78

Sam nodded. 'Gleason would be the best bet, I'd think. If it isn't him, I'd take a bet it was the Colfax brothers, Heller, or Duer. It could have been all four. They want to keep that ten-mile strip. They'll fight for it.'

'You call this fighting? Raiding a sleeping village in the middle of the night?'

Farley didn't answer that. The pair sat silently for several long moments. At last Burke said in a harsh, determined voice, 'It isn't going to happen, Sam. I'm not going to let it happen. They've been robbed and cheated and lied to ever since the first white man came out here. That strip means something to me, and it means even more to them. To me it means that maybe, at last, our government is going to start trying to be fair with the Indians. It means that to them, too, but it also means they can hunt again for a year or two. It means they can regain a little of their self-respect.'

Sam Farley stared at Burke's intent, still-angry face. Burke was one Indian Bureau employee who commanded his respect. Scrupulously honest, he understood the Cheyennes better, perhaps, than any white man alive. Not only that. He liked the Cheyennes. He respected them. Now Burke said, 'They can only be crowded so far, and they've been crowded as far as they're going to be. If we don't get the men who burned those lodges last night, it will prove to Angry Bear that no white man can be trusted to do right by them. You can see what alternative that leaves.'

Sam nodded. 'I can see all right.' He glanced up. 'Here comes Mart with the horses.'

He got up and so did Burke. When Mart reached them with the horses they mounted. Sam led out, heading north. Burke followed, and Mart brought up the rear.

Mart frowned as he rode. He'd hoped his talk with Angry Bear in the village on Horsetooth Creek might have done some good. At least he'd hoped the chief would consider the things he'd said. Now he knew there was little chance he had. Even now, Angry Bear's young men were probably following the raiders' trail.

He thought of Marian out at the Colfax place, and experienced a new concern. She wasn't safe out there with things the way they were. Her brothers might have been on the raid. They might have left a trail leading home.

Then he shook his head. Ed and Ben Colfax weren't that stupid. If they'd been going to leave a trail, they'd have left one to the Gleason ranch. That way they could revenge themselves on Max for beating Marian.

The miles dropped behind with a slowness that was maddening to Mart. Periodically his mind would chill with fear, remembering the atrocities that had been committed twenty years ago. Such a brief span of years didn't change the nature of the Cheyenne. It could happen again—at any time.

Burke was talking to Sam. 'I don't know why people are so damned unreasonable. This could be worked out fine, if they'd just try and work it out.'

'How?'

'Leasing. Cattle on that land wouldn't bother the Cheyenne. All they want is the hunting. They'd lease it back to the cattlemen, if they'd pay some kind of small lease fee.'

Sam snorted. 'I can see Otto Gleason paying a lease fee for something he figures is already his.'

Burke nodded. 'That's the trouble. Nobody even wants to try.'

Sam said, 'Gleason's wife and two daughters were murdered by the Cheyennes. Mrs. Colfax was kidnaped and held by them, and you know what that meant twenty years ago. Duer's permanently crippled from a Cheyenne arrow wound, and Heller lost the girl he was going to marry. None of 'em are likely to be reasonable with the Cheyennes. Not now. Not ever.'

They crossed the reservation boundary and pounded toward the village on Horsetooth Creek. It was afternoon when they arrived. They rode in slowly, deliberately.

Angry Bear approached, accompanied by a medicine man. Sam Farley raised a hand. Burke ranged up beside him. Mart could see the blackened ruins of the five tepees burned last night. He could feel the sullen anger in the

Indians that surrounded them.

Burke said, 'I have brought the sheriff, Angry Bear. He will trail the men who raided your village last night. He will see that they are punished.'

The tall chief's expression was cold, unrelenting. Burke asked, 'Did you get my message? About waiting until you heard from me?'

Angry Bear nodded coldly. His glance touched Mart accusingly.

'Have you waited? Have you kept your young men from taking up the trail?'

Again the cold eyes rested on Mart. He shook his head. 'My young men were angry. They have no patience with waiting for the white man's law to act.'

Mart felt a sinking sensation in his stomach. Sam Farley said, 'Circle the camp, Mart, and pick up the trail.'

Mart turned his horse and rode out of the village. He kicked the horse into a lope and circled the village. He found the kerosene cans where the raiders had left them. He picked up the trail leaving the village and got down from his horse.

There were shod hoofprints made by the raiders' horses last night. There were unshod hoofprints made by the young braves' horses at daylight today. He counted as accurately as he could, then rode back to where Sam and Burke were waiting for him. He said, 'About half a dozen braves took the trail early today, probably as soon as it was light.'

Sam said, 'All right. Let's go.'

Burke hesitated. 'I'm going to stay here, Sam. I'm going to try and talk some sense into them.'

Sam nodded. 'Tell them the raiders will be caught. Tell them the law will punish them. But tell them too that if their young men have done anything wrong, they will be punished too.'

Mart led them to where the trail began. Sam kicked his horse into a steady lope, with Mart keeping pace. They had gone no more than a couple of miles when Sam turned his head. 'It was Max all right. With that many men, it had to be.'

Mart said worriedly, 'He didn't even try to hide his trail. Do you suppose he laid an ambush for any bucks that might have followed him?'

Sam Farley shrugged, but his worried eyes told Mart he had considered it. He held his horse to a steady lope. The sun sank deliberately in the western sky.

They crossed the reservation boundary. The trail still led undeviatingly toward the Gleason place.

Mart frowned as he studied it. At last he said, 'Something puzzles me. These men were traveling pretty fast—like someone was chasing them. But no one was. How do you figure that?'

Sam said, 'Both Otto and Max hate Cheyennes. We know Otto can't ride, so it couldn't have been him that led this bunch. It had to be Max. Max hates Indians, but he's also afraid of them. He was probably half scared to death last night. That would explain him riding like he thought he was being chased. It would also explain why he didn't try to hide his trail.'

'The jail's going to be pretty full if you arrest the whole damn bunch.'

Sam Farley did not reply. The sun sank behind the broken land in the west. Its glow flamed briefly on a few high clouds.

Sam was pushing harder now, trying to beat the falling darkness to the Gleason ranch.

Both men were silent and intent. As the light faded, Sam Farley dropped back with the comment, 'Your eyes are better'n mine. You follow it.'

Mart forged ahead. It was still easy for him to read the trail. He'd learned trailing from the Cheyennes themselves. He'd be able to follow it so long as there was any light at all.

While yet a mile from Gleason's buildings, he dismounted and followed the trail on foot. Neither man doubted where the trail would lead. Yet Mart understood Sam's reason for following it all the way to Gleason's house. He had to have evidence that would hold up in court.

He stopped suddenly and turned his head. 'Trail forks here. The bucks veered off to the

84

right. Gleason's trail goes straight in.'

Sam said, 'I'll follow it. You take the Indians' trail for a little ways. I want to know why they veered away. Maybe they just wanted to know who raided their village and turned back when they'd made sure. But it could have been something else.'

Without answering, Mart took the trail of the unshod hoofs. Sam dismounted and slowly followed the other trail toward the ranch buildings three quarters of a mile away.

The Indians' trail was harder to read, and Mart frowned with concentration as he followed it. Half a mile fell behind.

Once he stopped and glanced toward the Gleason ranch. Lamplight flickered from the windows now. That was reassuring at least, he thought. And so was the direction this trail had taken so suddenly. At least there had been no raid by the Indians yet. At least no one had been killed.

His horse suddenly threw up his head and tugged rebelliously at the reins. Mart turned his head and looked at the animal.

Ears pricked, the horse was watching something off to the right. In the darkness all Mart could see was a blob of something dark against the lighter plain.

He turned and walked toward it, without releasing the horse's reins. Before he had reached it, he knew what it was.

A steer, already beginning to bloat. There

was an arrow sticking out of the dead animal's neck. And now, from here, others were visible. He counted five in all.

He mounted and turned his horse's head toward the lights of the Gleason place. The Indians hadn't attacked the house, but they'd had their revenge anyway. For each tepee, a steer. Five tepees burned. Five steers killed.

They'd done it in daylight too. They'd done it in plain sight of the Gleason ranch. He couldn't help smiling wryly to himself at their doing so.

The young bucks had their revenge for the burned tepees. They had also warned the whites. An eye for an eye; a tooth for a tooth.

He galloped away toward the ranch, and caught Sam Farley a hundred yards short of it. He said, 'There's five dead steers out there in plain sight of this place. There's an arrow in the neck of each.'

Sam Farley uttered an angry curse. He said, 'All right, Mart. Let's go do what we've got to do.'

CHAPTER NINE

For an instant, Mart held his horse motionless. He stared at Sam Farley's face, trying to make out its expression in the darkness. At last he asked, 'Who are you going to take? Max or

Otto?'

'Max led the raid.'

'But Otto gave the order for it. Max wouldn't have done it on his own.'

'Fact remains. Max did it.'

Mart was silent for a moment. He still got angry whenever he thought of Max manhandling Marian the way he had. He realized that he wanted more satisfaction from Max than the fight had given him. He wanted Max in jail. But he also realized that jailing Max wouldn't put an end to the trouble that was shaping up. Otto could still order his men to make raids against the Cheyennes. He didn't need his son for that.

He said, 'If you want to stop trouble with the Indians . . . you'd better jail Otto instead of Max. But if you want to get back at Max for the way he treated Marian, and, I have to admit, I'd like that too, then Max is the man we want.'

Sam Farley grunted, 'All right. We'll take Otto then.' There was satisfaction in his voice.

Riding in at the sheriff's side, Mart grinned wryly to himself. Sam hadn't intended taking Max. He'd just been sounding out his deputy— to see whether Mart could separate his personal feelings from his sense of responsibility toward his job.

They halted their horses at the back door of the house. Mart swung stiffly from his horse. The pitchfork wound still pained him considerably whenever he put weight on the leg. Right now he felt the warmth of blood on the bandage. Today's exertion had started it bleeding again, but he knew bleeding was good for it. It would carry out any infection that might be developing.

Sam Farley pounded heavily on the door. Della Chavez answered it, and Farley asked, 'Otto still up?'

She nodded and stood aside. Farley went in and Mart followed him. Della led them across the kitchen and into the parlor beyond. Otto was sitting in a chair, glaring at his son who stood in the center of the room.

Max scowled at Mart. Sam Farley said, 'Tell Max to hitch a horse to your buggy, Otto. You're under arrest for that raid on the village on Horsetooth Creek.'

Otto looked at him innocently. 'Me? You know damn well I can't ride a horse.'

'You can give orders though. Next time Max makes a raid like that, tell him to hide his trail. It led straight here.'

'If you're so smart following trail—how come you didn't see those five dead steers?'

'Mart saw 'em. I'd say you came off pretty light. A lodge means a hell of a lot more to a Cheyenne than a steer does to you.'

'Them five ain't the first.'

'What do you mean, they ain't the first?'

'Why the hell do you think I told Max to lead that raid? He found a steer north of here

88

with an arrow in it yesterday.'

Sam Farley stared down at him disgustedly. 'You're a fool, Otto. You ought to know how these things go. They kill a steer, so you burn five of their lodges. Then they kill five more steers. What were you planning to do to them for that? Kill some of them? And what did you think they'd do to you in return?' His expression of disgust deepened. 'You were here at the time of the trouble twenty years ago. Your ranch was burned, and your wife and daughters killed in retaliation for something someone had done to the Cheyennes. Someone you probably didn't even know.'

Otto's face turned gray. His eyes burned at Sam. Max's face was also pale, but his eyes wouldn't meet either Sam's or Mart's.

Sam said implacably, 'Max, go hitch the buggy up.'

Max looked at his father questioningly. A fleeting expression of disgust crossed Otto's hard old face. He nodded at Max almost imperceptibly.

Max hurried from the room. Otto grunted sourly, 'The yellow pup!'

Sam's eyes were narrowed, hard. 'Why is he a yellow pup? Because he's scared of the Cheyennes? You can't blame Max for that; he was only a kid when your place was burned. He saw things no kid should have to see—his own mother and sisters . . .'

Otto Gleason's voice was an incoherent roar. 'Shut up, God damn you! Shut up!'

Mart stared at him. Otto's face was congested with blood. Great veins stood out darkly on his forehead. His eyes were tortured, but they were also alive with hate.

Sam continued mercilessly, 'Do you want to see it happen again? Is that what you're working toward? Don't think that because the Indians are dirty and sullen and beaten these days that they can't do it all over again. They hate us even more than we hate them because they lost. They lost and we won.'

'They ain't going to get an inch of land from me!'

Sam stared at him disgustedly. 'You're a bigger fool than I thought you were, if you believe that. The government says it belongs to them. That's the end of it.'

'The hell it is!'

Sam looked at Mart helplessly. Mart shook his head. Max came into the house and looked at the three of them sullenly. 'It's hitched.'

Sam said, 'Get whatever you want to take, Otto.'

Without looking at his son, Otto said, 'Get me my razor and a change of clothes.'

Max left the room.

Mart waited, troubled by the notion that this had been too easy. Uneasiness began to increase in him. He heard the back door of the house open and close stealthily.

He glanced at Otto. The old man's eyes were bright, and there was a triumphant smile on his hard, thin mouth.

Sam said softly, 'Tell him to forget it, Otto. Send Della after him and tell him to forget it.'

'Forget what?'

'You know what. Max just sneaked out of the house.'

'I didn't hear anything.'

Sam shrugged wearily, crossed the room, and blew out the lamp. He said, 'Mart, pick him up and carry him outside.'

Mart felt his way across the darkened room to Otto's chair. He picked up chair and all, surprised at the old man's lack of weight. Awkwardly he carried him toward the door.

Sam went out first, gun in hand. He said softly as Mart brought Otto out, 'Yell to him Otto. Unless you want somebody getting hurt.'

'You go to hell!'

Sam murmured, 'Put the chair down beside the buggy, Mart, and lift him in.'

Mart crossed to where the buggy stood. He put the chair down and lifted Otto in. There was no sound out in the darkness, but the lamps in the bunkhouse were out and the place was dark.

Mart drew his gun. Warily, he walked toward his horse. He couldn't guess what Max had in mind, but he knew that a frightened man is dangerous. Max was scared, and might do anything.

91

The shot came suddenly but not unexpectedly. Mart started violently and swung around, too late to catch the flash. He called, 'You all right, Sam?'

'I'm all right.'

A cold chill began creeping over Mart. There was no way of telling how many men were hidden by darkness out there. There was no way of telling what they were going to do. Otto bawled suddenly, 'Give 'em hell, son!'

Another gun flared in the night. This time Mart was ready. He sprinted toward the flash, bending low, weaving back and forth as he ran. The flash came again, so close when it did that Mart smelled the powder smoke.

He didn't think Max was trying to hit him, but you could never be sure about a thing like that. He figured Max was still running scared. He didn't want them to arrest Otto instead of him. He didn't want to be free, still subject to Otto's orders from the jail. The jail represented safety to Max, because the Cheyennes couldn't get him there.

Mart covered the last half dozen feet in a flying dive that sent him crashing against the shooter's legs. The man went down, with Mart clawing forward, trying to get his hands on the gun.

Behind him, he could hear some kind of movement, but he paid no attention to it. He got his hands on the gun and wrenched it violently. It came free and the man cursed, and instantly Mart knew it was Max he was grappling with.

There was no more shooting now, but he heard Sam Farley's voice bawl angrily, 'Get back in the bunkhouse, every goddam one of you! Ten seconds from now I'm going to start shooting at everything that moves!'

Max stopped fighting suddenly. He said breathlessly, 'All right, Mart. All right!'

Mart disengaged himself and stood up. He leaned down, seized Max's arm, and yanked him to his feet. He gave him a vicious push in the direction of the buggy.

And now he understood what the flurry of movement had been. Max had deliberately shot the buggy horse. He lay on his side against one of the shafts, both of which now rested on the ground.

A lamp flickered in the bunkhouse. By its light, Mart could see the men trooping in through the open door.

Sam Farley said disgustedly, 'Pick up your father and take him back inside.'

Max lifted his father out of the buggy and carried him into the house. He put him down in the chair, which Mart had carried in after him. Sam came in, re-lighted the lamp, and stared at Max disgustedly. 'That was a stupid business. What did you think you were going to accomplish by it?'

There was a hooded look of triumph in Max's eyes. Sam said angrily, 'All right. All right! We'll take you instead of him. Is that what you wanted?'

Max didn't reply. Nor did he look at his father.

Sam said, 'Take him out, Mart, and saddle up a horse for him. I'm not going to fool around getting the harness off that buggy horse. We'll come back out and get Otto tomorrow when it's light.'

Mart looked at Max. Max headed for the door, and Mart followed him. Outside in the darkness, Mart said softly, 'I'm just going to tell you once. Pull any other fancy stunts and I'll put an egg on your head that won't go away for a week.'

Max didn't reply, but his movements were careful and deliberate. He led the way to the barn. Just inside the door, he stopped and lighted a lantern. He put it down and went to one of the stalls for a horse. He saddled quickly, then led the horse toward Mart.

Mart took the reins. 'Walk ahead of me.'

Max headed for the house, with Mart following. Mart said, 'That was pretty cute. You wanted to go to jail, didn't you? You wanted to be where the Indians couldn't get to you.'

Max didn't reply. He stopped sullenly just outside the kitchen door. Mart was thinking that Max, having tried to impress his father once, might do it again. He kept his eyes steadily on the man.

94

Sam Farley came to the door. Seeing Mart and his prisoner, he came outside. He glanced toward the bunkhouse. 'Wait a minute, Mart. I've got a few things to say to Otto's crew.'

He crossed the yard to the bunkhouse, opened the door, and went inside. Mart could hear every word he said.

'Max is going to jail for leading that raid last night. As it stands now, those of you who were with him probably won't be charged with anything because you were following orders. But just bear in mind one thing—kill one of those Cheyennes and whoever's involved will go to trial.'

He paused. None of the Gleason's crew members said anything. Sam said, 'And it won't make a damn bit of difference who fires the fatal shot. Everybody involved will be equally guilty. Have I made that clear?'

There was a rumble of sullen assent. Sam came to the door. From there he said disgustedly, 'Everybody's been acting pretty stupid up to now. I hope a few of you start showing you've got a little sense.'

He came striding across the yard. He swung heavily to his horse. Mart nodded at Max, who swung to his saddle.

Sam Farley led out toward town, with Max following. Mart mounted and fell in behind Max.

Things seemed to be under control, he thought. But he could not rid himself of his uneasiness. Sam had been right when he'd said everybody had been acting stupidly. Mart could see no reason why any of them should suddenly start showing that they had some sense. He glanced behind uneasily.

CHAPTER TEN

They rode in silence for a long, long time. Max stared straight ahead, scowling into the darkness furiously. There was a feeling of desperation in him and a smoldering anger that would not go away.

He had bungled the raid on the village of Angry Bear. Because he had been afraid, he had led them straight home when he could easily have done otherwise. He could have taken the men into Medicine Lodge, where the Indians could not follow. From there, he could have sent them home separately. It would have been so simple had he been thinking straight.

But he hadn't been thinking straight. He had been scared half to death. Riding home from the village on Horsetooth Creek all that had been in his mind had been a memory of three naked, mutilated bodies lying in front of a burned-out ranch. That and a panicky fear that they were being pursued.

Furthermore, he had bungled tonight. And

again it had been because he was afraid. He had meant to erase the previous failure and raise his father's opinion of him. Instead, he had earned his father's contempt and disgust. His father was convinced he had stirred up that ruckus just to get himself arrested and thrown into jail where he would be safe.

Worst of all, his father was right. He faced the fact that he had been dishonest with himself. He had convinced himself that by resisting the sheriff and his deputy, he was trying to erase a failure and raise his father's opinion of him when in reality he was only trying to get himself arrested and thrown in jail.

He thought of Marian Colfax, and a sudden feeling of nausea crawled in his stomach. He hated her for what he believed her to be, yet he was also ashamed of the way he had beaten her.

Uncertain and confused, he stared at the sheriff's broad back ahead of him. The only light was that shed by the brilliant stars. There was no moon.

He turned his head and stared at Mart, riding ten or fifteen feet behind. He hated Mart almost as savagely as he hated the Cheyennes. Mart had humiliated him by beating him in front of his father and the crew. Mart had humiliated him again tonight.

His head sank forward onto his chest. More than anything else in the world, he wanted his father to approve of him. But that was impossible now. Sam Farley was going to put him in jail and there he'd stay until this trouble was over with. He'd have no chance to prove anything. He'd feel the searing burn of his father's contempt for as long as Otto lived.

Suddenly, the injustice of it made him furious. Otto had been a grown man at the time of the massacre. He'd been only a boy. Otto blamed him for his fear but hell, any kid who'd seen what he had would have been afraid.

Seething inwardly, he considered spurring his horse and trying to get away from the sheriff and his deputy. He abandoned the idea almost immediately. He couldn't get away from this pair. He wouldn't have a chance. They'd overtake him, drop a rope over him, and dump him from his horse.

But he could try, he thought. Even if there was no chance of success, he could try. Otto would hear of it and give him credit for trying at least . . .

Sourly he exposed his own dishonesty with himself. He didn't really want to get away and knew it was impossible. He just wanted Otto to believe he'd tried.

He faced a bleak future suddenly. How was he going to live with himself, knowing he was a coward, knowing he could not even be honest with himself? How would he face Otto's contempt and his own self-contempt this year, the next, and the year after that?

He wished that he was dead. In this moment, he would almost have welcomed a horde of attacking, screaming Cheyennes.

But raw terror touched him instantly when he heard the dim, distant sounds of galloping hoofs from behind. Sam Farley cursed and immediately spurred his horse into a lope. Max kept pace and could hear Mart pounding along behind. For a while, the sounds of pursuit were lost in the sounds of their own horses' galloping hoofs.

The sheriff jumped his horse recklessly into a deep, dry wash. He dismounted instantly, and caught the bridle of Max's horse as he jumped into the wash after him. Mart nearly rammed the two of them with his horse, but reined aside in time.

The sheriff had a rifle in his hands. He pushed Max against the near wall of the wash with the curt command, 'Stay down. Don't try to get away or I'll put a knot on the top of your head.'

The thunder of approaching hoofs was louder now. Mart came up on Max's other side, a revolver in his hand. Max peered into the darkness fearfully. He had wished for pursuit by a band of Cheyennes. It looked like he might have gotten his wish.

But it was not Indians that materialized out of the darkness. Nor was it an Indian voice that bawled, 'Farley! Turn Max loose. Turn him loose and there won't be any trouble.'

Farley's reply was a carefully placed rifle shot that dumped the horse out from under one of the milling riders fifty yards away. The rest scattered, fading back into darkness and spreading out.

Max glanced aside at Farley. The sheriff had a rifle in his hands. His revolver was strapped around his waist. He turned his head and looked at Mart. Mart's revolver was in his hand but his rifle . . .

Almost stealthily, Max turned around and stared at Mart's horse. He thought he could see the rifle stock sticking out of the boot. The horse was standing no more than fifteen feet away.

Out in the darkness, now, guns flared from half a dozen widely separated points. Bullets struck the ground at the lip of the wash, scattering dirt, and then ricocheting off into space, whining like angry bees.

Mart's horse with the rifle on it was fifteen feet away. It might have been fifteen miles, for all the chance Max had of reaching it. The minute he moved they'd have their guns on him.

But he *had* to get away. It was the only chance he had left of changing his father's opinion of him. If he could get away . . . Maybe he could force himself to be what his father wanted him to be. Maybe he could force himself to face up to the Cheyennes.

The firing slackened in the darkness out there. Both the sheriff and his deputy poked their heads over the lip of the wash and opened up.

For an instant the wash was filled with sound, with powder smoke, and the two were intent on trying to pick targets out of nearly complete darkness in front of them.

Silently, stealthily, Max eased back down the steep bank of the wash. He reached the bottom before either of them turned. He was on his feet and moving toward Mart's horse when the sheriff roared, 'Max! Damn you . . . !'

He lunged for the horse, but the animal spooked away. Frantically Max ran after him.

He got his hands on the rifle stock. He yanked it clear. The pull of it dragged him off his feet and threw him to his knees. The horse trotted down the wash.

Sam Farley fired a shot into the air. 'Drop it, Max! The next one's going in your gut!'

Max levered the rifle frantically. He leveled it at Sam and pulled the trigger.

The roar of the gun from the bottom of the wash filled it with roaring sound. Smoke billowed out toward Sam. He straightened up convulsively, then lost his footing and rolled to the sandy bottom of the wash.

Mart snapped a shot at Max, and the bullet burned his thigh. Max turned and ran down the wash, dodging and zigzagging. Another shot ripped out, but this one missed.

He ran for a couple of hundred yards until he found a place where he could scramble out of the wash. Once out, he got to his feet and yelled, 'Hey! It's Max! Over here!'

A man galloped toward him. Reaching him, the man pulled his foot out of the left stirrup and Max swung up behind. The man dug in his spurs, and the horse thundered away. He had gone no more than a quarter mile before the others converged on him. All headed back toward home.

The men were yelling at him, laughing and congratulating him, but Max felt worse than he had before. He'd shot Sam Farley and if the sheriff died he'd hang for it. Even Otto Gleason couldn't save him from that. Nothing could save him if the sheriff died.

At least, he thought, his father couldn't accuse him of having no guts. At least he couldn't accuse him of that any more.

He felt as though he had already been condemned.

*   *   *

Back in the wash, Mart Leathers cursed softly, steadily, as he knelt at the sheriff's side. Sam Farley lay on his back, a leg twisted beneath him. Mart straightened it out unthinkingly. He asked, 'Sam, where are you hit? Is it bad?'

It was a moment before the sheriff answered him, a moment that seemed an eternity to Mart. When the sheriff's voice came, it was weak and strained with pain. 'Chest. Right side. It ain't good, boy.'

Mart fumbled for a match. He struck it on the sole of his boot and by its light looked at the sheriff's face, then at his chest. There was a spreading spot of blood on Sam's shirt-front, and his face was almost gray. Mart said, 'You need Doc, Sam, and fast.'

The sheriff's voice was so weak it was hard to hear. 'Help me on my horse.'

Mart got to his feet. He walked to where Farley's horse stood, picked up the reins, and led him back. He said worriedly, 'Maybe I ought to hightail it to town and get a wagon.'

'No time for that. Help me up.'

Mart lifted him to his feet. Suddenly he was scared—worse scared than he had ever been in his life before. Sam Farley got a foot into the stirrup, and Mart heaved him up onto the horse, steadying him afterward until Sam said faintly, 'I'm all right now.'

'Want me to tie you on?'

'Huh uh. I'm all right.' Farley spoke between clenched teeth.

Mart walked along the wash to where the other two horses stood. Swiftly he unsaddled the one Max Gleason had ridden and turned him loose. He mounted his own horse and rode back to Sam.

Leaning low, he gathered up the reins. 'Anytime you want to stop, Sam, sing out.'

'Uh huh.' Sam was holding onto the saddle horn. Mart led his horse along the wash for almost a quarter mile until he found a sloping bank where he could ride out of it. Here, he suddenly realized how impossible it would be for Sam to hold on while his horse climbed out of the wash. He dismounted and climbed up behind Sam. Leading his own horse, he rode up out of the wash.

This way, he continued on toward town, forcing the horse to maintain a smooth, running walk.

Sam's head lolled forward. Mart didn't know whether he was conscious or not, but he could feel the slow, steady beat of Sam's heart.

The distance to town seemed endless to him. Terror was like an icy hand closed around his heart. If Sam Farley died . . .

He admitted that Sam didn't have much chance. A man shot in the chest, forced to ride more than twenty miles . . .

He began to think of Max. There were three kinds of men, he decided ruefully. Those like Otto, whose courage was unquestioned, who could be counted upon to fight, no matter what. There was another kind, who never fought, who would retreat every time, and who could be counted upon to retreat. The third kind was the most dangerous of all, because you never knew what to expect of them. Max was one of these. Max was afraid, but he could not admit he was, nor could he retreat and live with himself afterward. So he was driven to stupid, foolish things, like shooting Sam tonight.

The hours passed. Sam Farley lost consciousness and regained it again. Once he asked weakly, 'Where are we, Mart?'

'Almost there, Sam.'

Shortly afterward, he saw the dark buildings in front of him. He rode up the street, dark and silent at this time of night. He halted before Doc Williams' box-like house.

He slid out of the saddle, steadying Sam as he did. He let Sam slide gently out of the saddle into his arms.

Carrying him, staggering, he kicked open the gate, and went up the walk to the house. He kicked on the door.

Almost instantly he heard a sleepy roar, 'For Christ's sake, cut it out! I'm coming!'

A lamp flickered behind the door and it opened. Mart said, 'It's Sam, Doc. He's been shot.'

Doc held the door. He wore a nightshirt, and his hair was mussed. He said, 'Lay him down on that table there.'

Mart laid Sam down. Doc grabbed his glasses and pinched them to his nose. He grabbed a pair of scissors and immediately began to cut Sam's shirt away from the wound. Mart watched worriedly. Once he said, 'Did I do right, bringing him in, Doc? Or should I have left him and come for a wagon?'

It was a moment before Doc answered him. Then, as though suddenly understanding how important the question was to Mart, he turned his head. 'You did right, Mart. You did right. He'd have been dead by the time you got back with the wagon.'

Mart asked nervously, 'Will he . . . ?'

Doc's voice was patient. 'I can't tell yet. You go on home and get some sleep. I'll do the best I can.'

'Hadn't I better stay, in case you need some help?'

'I won't need help. Now get on out of here.'

Reluctantly, Mart went out the door. He mounted one of the horses and, leading the other one, headed for the stable down the street.

Even if Sam Farley recovered, he thought, he'd be in bed for weeks. It would be days before Sam even knew what was going on.

The law was in Mart's hands now. And he was all alone.

CHAPTER ELEVEN

Ben and Ed Colfax had been gone most of the time since Marian's beating. Though she was ashamed of herself for feeling so, she was glad that they were gone. Meeting their eyes was difficult. Carrying on a normal conversation was impossible. Always, between them, was the wall erected by Max Gleason when he had called her Indian.

A thousand times she had asked herself if it was true. And a thousand times she had failed to come up with an answer that would satisfy her. She just didn't know. There was no way to tell. Her mother had been taken in December, but it was possible that she had already been pregnant. It was also possible that she had not.

This morning, she cleaned house almost frantically, as though by working she could stop her thoughts. When the house was spotless, she began to wash. Hanging the clothes out on the line, she thought of Mart.

And now, for the first time, her face softened. Her eyes filled with tears. Mart was so good. Unlike Max, he didn't care one way or the other. He didn't care if she was half Indian or not.

She wished he hadn't gone away when he had, wished he had not had to take that prisoner to Deer Lodge when he had. If he'd stayed . . . she might have gotten to know him better, might never have let herself become engaged to Max.

She'd thought she knew Max, but now she realized she'd never known him. Even growing up with him, going to school with him, she hadn't gotten to know him thoroughly. She hadn't thought him capable of beating a woman the way he'd beaten her.

She went back into the house and fixed herself something to eat, but she ate very little of it. Because she had suddenly come to a decision about her heritage. She couldn't live the rest of her life in doubt. She had to know. And there was only one place she could find out anything. On the Cheyenne reservation. In the Cheyenne villages.

With her decision made, she left the house quickly, crossed the yard to the corral, and went inside. She took down a rope from a nail and shook out a loop. Almost as expertly as a man, she sent the loop sailing out to settle over the head of the horse she wanted to ride.

She coiled the rope and led the horse to the gate, where she bridled him. Saddling was quick and deft, but the preoccupied look never left her face. She mounted and rode toward the reservation boundary without looking back.

It was a strange day. The skies were overcast with thin, high clouds. What sunlight filtered through them was weak and faint.

A depressing day, of neither rain nor sun. Something about a day like this always made her feel moody and blue, and she suddenly wondered why, smiling ruefully at herself.

Perhaps, she thought, another day like this was connected in her mind with some minor unhappiness so long ago it had faded back into the dim recesses of her memory.

She reached the boundary of the ten-mile

strip that was being returned to the Cheyennes, and started across. Everywhere there were cattle, some belonging to her brothers, some belonging to the other ranchers who used the strip. And as she rode she began to feel uneasiness, almost hopelessness at the difficulties involved in finding out what she had to know.

In the first place, the Cheyennes didn't like to talk to whites. They distrusted them. In the second ... what had happened had been twenty years ago. If her father was, indeed, a Cheyenne, it was probable that he was dead. Or he had forgotten. Or he simply would not talk.

Half a dozen times she halted her horse, on the point of going back. Each time she went on again, her face a little more determined than it had been before. Once it occurred to her that her brothers might return, find her gone, and grow worried about her. They might find the trail she had made leaving home. They might follow and do something foolish or dangerous.

She began to hurry, kicking her horse in the sides with her heels. The horse broke into a trot, then into a lope. Slowly the miles dropped behind.

Marian had never been this far north before. She did not know exactly where the reservation boundary was. Neither did she know where their villages were located. But she did know one thing. Their villages would all be located on the banks of streams. All she had to do was find a stream and follow it.

She reached Horsetooth Creek several miles southeast of the village of Angry Bear. Hesitating as to which direction to go, she finally turned north and west, studying the ground as she rode.

There were many horsetracks here, all unshod, mostly heading in the same direction she was. Several times she passed a loose band of horses. Scattered among each band were pintos, spotted horses of black and white or brown and white. Pintos were highly valued by the Indians.

It was well into the afternoon before she brought the village into sight. She halted immediately, wishing she had not come, knowing suddenly how useless it really was. There were twenty or thirty such villages scattered over the Cheyenne reservation. It would be impossible for her to visit all of them. It would be impossible to talk to all the old men who might have ridden on those raids twenty years ago.

Then her mouth firmed with determination. She was here. At least she would do what she could.

She rode into the village, seeing the blackened ruins of the burned tepees. She halted her horse uncertainly.

Women and children stopped what they were doing to stare at her. Their faces were impassive, curious. Yet there was a quality in them that defeated the impassiveness. It was hostility, visible in their glittering eyes. It was distrust and dislike, and it showed itself in their thinned-out mouths.

A old woman finally approached her and said, 'What you want? What you do here? You go! Go now!'

'I want to see your chief.'

'Angry Bear got no time for paleface woman.'

Marian dismounted from her horse. 'I want to see him anyway.'

More women collected, jabbering at her in a mixture of English and Cheyenne. A couple of dogs arrived and began to snap at her heels.

Suddenly she heard a man's voice shout. The women dispersed, dragging the children along with them. The dogs slunk away behind the nearest lodge.

A man approached Marian, an elderly man with hard old eyes and a weathered, ancient face. This had to be Angry Bear, she thought, and was suddenly at a loss for words. She couldn't talk to this old man about what had happened twenty years ago, she realized. It would be wasted breath. Even if he knew anything, which was doubtful, he wasn't going to talk about it.

Marian said, 'I got lost. I saw your village and . . .' She stopped. Tears misted her vision and she brushed them angrily away. She looked at the man and said, 'Max Gleason said I was half Indian. I want to know if it is true. My mother was taken by Cheyennes twenty years ago. She was rescued later. I want to talk to the men who took her.'

The old chief stared at her impassively. He shook his head. Marian couldn't tell whether he meant he did not understand or whether he was telling her he knew nothing about the incident.

She said, 'Please. What I want to know will hurt no one.'

He continued to stare at her coldly. She knew he understood. His understanding was there in his eyes. But his expression did not change, and he finally said, 'You go. You not belong here. You trouble for Cheyenne.'

Her shoulders slumped. She should have known better than to come here in the first place. She should have realized how enormous, how impossible the task would be. Her mother was not the only white woman who had been kidnaped twenty years before. The kidnaping and rape of a white woman had not even been an important incident to these people then. Even if they would talk about it, they probably wouldn't remember it. She nodded dispiritedly. 'All right. I'll go.'

The old chief nodded, but an unexpected hesitation had come into his face. He glanced around, as though looking for someone. When he looked back at Marian, there was plain worry in his eyes. He spoke to a boy standing nearby, and the boy trotted swiftly away.

Angry Bear said, 'Not safe—white woman ride alone. Angry Bear go with white woman. Young men angry about burned tepees.' He gestured toward the charred remains of the five tepees.

Marian started to protest, then stopped herself. What the chief had said was true, she supposed, even if she hadn't thought of it. She asked, 'Who burned the tepees?'

'White men burn. Come in night.'

'I hope you don't think my brothers . . .'

'Not brothers. Gleason.'

The boy trotted up, leading a horse for the chief. Angry Bear leaped astride and motioned for Marian to mount. She did, and the chief led away toward the south.

He rode swiftly, his moccasin-clad heels drumming against the horse's sides. Mostly, the horse ran or loped. Occasionally he would slow to a trot.

Marian felt cold when she thought of what might have happened to her. But she hadn't known about the burned tepees. She hadn't known any trouble had started between the reservation Cheyennes and the whites. If she had, she certainly wouldn't have come. She was not a fool.

No wonder her reception at the Cheyenne village had been so cold, she thought, and she remembered seeing no young men at the village on Horsetooth Creek. Even now, they might be attacking Gleason's ranch. She stared at the thin, strong back of the chief ahead of her.

She felt a sudden compassion for the fierce old man that surprised her. She frowned, realizing she ought to hate the chief, ought to hate all Cheyennes the way her brothers did. They had, after all, kidnaped her mother. They had undoubtedly mistreated her cruelly. Angry Bear might even have been one of those who kidnaped her.

But she couldn't help feeling sorry for him. Because he was all alone, one of a beaten race trying desperately now to prevent open warfare with the whites, warfare he knew must end in further humiliation and defeat for the Cheyennes. Accompanying her was not an act of concern for her safety. He only knew that if she was molested by young men of his tribe, there would be no avoiding the swift and terrible retaliation that would follow.

The sun dropped toward the horizon in the west, visible through the thin layer of clouds as a luminescent ball. Again the uneasiness caused by the day came over Marian. It was almost as though she knew something was going to happen, something terrible that would affect her and those she loved.

Angry Bear did not look back at her. Nor did he speak. But occasionally, when she dropped slightly behind, he would slow his

114

horse until she caught up.

She began to feel a strange, unexplainable kinship with the taciturn old man. What did it really matter, she thought, what her heritage was? She was who she was, what she was. Nothing could change that. Her brothers loved her, and while it might trouble them occasionally wondering if what Max had said was true, it would not affect their love.

Nor did Mart Leathers care. He had made it plain that it didn't matter to him whether she was half Cheyenne or not. Mart had been raised with the Indians, and he respected them, liked them too.

In late afternoon, they came in sight of the Colfax ranch. Here, Angry Bear stopped. He turned his head and looked at her. 'You safe now.'

She nodded. 'Thank you,' she said automatically, even though she knew he had not brought her home out of concern for her.

Angry Bear did not reply. He stared at her coldly. Silently he reined his horse aside and rode deliberately away. He held the horse to a walk, not looking back.

Marian stared after him for a long, long time. Then, with an expression that was almost sad, she reined her horse toward the house.

Briefly, the sun broke through the cloud cover and laid a bright orange light upon the land. But the pain of sadness did not leave Marian's eyes.

It was sadness for the Cheyennes, pity that had been stirred by the proud, fierce demeanor of the old chief who had spoken scarcely more than a dozen words to her.

They were the dispossessed, she thought suddenly. The Indians had been defenders of their lands twenty years ago; the whites, invaders who had come to steal what did not belong to them.

It was a distinction few white people bothered to think about. Because the Indian was different, ignorant by white standards, they took the stand he was not entitled to his land. Because he did not put the land to the same use the whites would put it to, they felt they had the right to take it away from him.

Marian reached the house, a shine of tears in her eyes. Never again, she thought, would she wonder about her heritage. Because now she didn't care. Indian blood in her veins, if it was there, was no different than her own white blood. A person might, she thought, even be proud of it.

CHAPTER TWELVE

Mart returned the horses to the livery barn after leaving Sam Farley at Doc's. The place was deserted and dark, so he unsaddled them and turned them into the corral out back. He caught a fresh horse for himself, saddled, then mounted and rode up the street to the jail.

He tied the horse out front, went in, and lighted the lamp. He began to pace nervously back and forth, scowling angrily to himself.

Damn! Neither he nor Sam had expected anything quite so foolish from Max. Both of them had known Max wanted to be arrested and thrown in jail. It hadn't been reasonable—what Max did.

But a scared man isn't reasonable, Mart thought ruefully. A scared man is liable to do anything. And Max Gleason was still scared. Maybe he was worse scared now than he had ever been.

He crossed the room to the old, cracked mirror over the wash basin and stared at himself sadly. Max wasn't the only one who was scared. He was scared himself. Thank God it didn't show.

He was scared of being alone, of trying to keep the peace without Sam Farley to tell him what to do. He was scared the whole thing would get completely out of hand and that he would fail.

He wasn't afraid of Max Gleason, though, and he wasn't afraid of Otto. And there was only one thing he could do. Come morning, he had to go out to the Gleason ranch. He had to arrest Max and bring him in to jail. That and only that would preserve the authority of the law.

Once his mind was made up, Mart found it possible to relax. He sat down in the sheriff's swivel chair and made himself a cigarette. He puffed thoughtfully. He guessed he wasn't nearly as afraid of what might happen as he was of uncertainty.

He wondered how Sam Farley was. He hesitated about going up to Doc's and finding out, then discarded the idea. Doc wouldn't know anything yet. It hadn't been half an hour since he'd left Doc's place.

The thing to do now was to get some sleep. He finished his cigarette, got up, and blew out the lamp. He crossed the room to the office couch and sank down on it. He closed his eyes.

He thought of Marian, and felt his anger at Max renew itself. He thought of the way Sam had looked, so pale and lifeless on Doc's table a while ago. Then he slept, the deep, dreamless sleep of exhaustion and did not awake until the sun came up.

He got up immediately, crossed the room to the wash-stand, and washed. He ran a comb through his hair, crammed on his hat, and went outside. He untied the horse, mounted, and rode up the street to Doc's.

The door was open. Doc was standing in the doorway, stretching. Mart asked, 'How is he?' half afraid of what Doc's answer was going to be.

'Holding on, Mart. That's about all I can say. But the longer he holds on, the better

118

chance he's got.'

Mart nodded, and Doc asked, 'Who shot him?'

'Max.' He hesitated a moment, then asked, 'Anything I can do?'

Doc shook his head. Mart reined his horse around and headed out of town. He headed north.

Riding, he wondered what he'd face when he got to Gleason's ranch. Would Otto try and protect Max? He doubted it. Otto, in spite of his acidity, liked Sam Farley and always had. He was probably thoroughly disgusted with his son for what he'd done. And he had sense enough to know he wouldn't help Max by taking on the law in his behalf.

The miles dropped away slowly behind. It was midmorning when Mart brought the Gleason place in sight.

It seemed to doze in the morning sun. Otto was sitting in his accustomed place on the porch. Della Chavez was hanging clothes on the clothesline in the yard. Mart saw a man working with a horse in the corral. Otherwise, the place seemed deserted.

He rode straight to the porch where Otto sat. He stared down, hostility in his eyes. Otto asked, 'How's Sam?'

'He's alive, no thanks to Max. Or he was when I left town. He's shot in the chest, and Doc won't say whether he's going to make it or not.'

Otto didn't speak, and there was genuine regret in his face. Mart said, 'What the hell did you expect, anyway, when you sent your crew after us last night?'

'I didn't want anybody to be hurt.' Otto wouldn't look at him.

Mart said, 'I've come for Max. Where is he?'

Anger touched Otto's eyes and thinned his mouth. He said, 'Gone. He left at daylight.'

Mart stared at the crippled old man, who had made bitterness and hatred so much a part of his life. Otto was blaming Max now, but the blame didn't belong with Max. It belonged squarely with Otto himself. He nodded, knowing he would waste his breath if he tried telling Otto this. He turned his horse and rode out.

He headed straight north until he was a quarter mile from the house. Then he began a circle, watching the ground closely as he rode.

Many trails led away from the Gleason ranch. Some had been made this morning. To most of them, Mart gave only scant attention, because he knew exactly what he was looking for—the trail of a hard-ridden horse. Max wouldn't have ridden away in a leisurely manner. He'd have ridden as though the devil was close on his heels.

He made a three-quarter circle before he found the trail he sought. When he did, he turned into it and lifted his horse to a steady lope.

Max had at least a ten-mile lead, he guessed, and he was heading south. He had to be headed for Duer's place.

Once he had made his guess as to Max's destination, Mart abandoned the trail. He put his horse into a direct line between where he now was and Duer's place. He forced the animal into a steady lope.

He reached Duer's in midafternoon. Sally Duer came to the door as he rode into the yard.

She was about twenty-five, full bodied, and blonde. She came out of the house, pushing back a wisp of hair from her forehead and smiling at him. 'Hello Mart. What brings you 'way out here?'

'I'm looking for Max Gleason. Has he been here?' He expected her to lie to him and watched her face closely as he spoke.

'Him! I haven't seen him for a week almost. But get down and come in. I've got some coffee on.' Her eyes were warm and personal.

He shook his head. 'I've got to find Max. He shot Sam Farley last night.'

He frowned thoughtfully at her. He'd gotten the feeling a moment ago that she was telling the truth—that she hadn't seen Max. It didn't seem likely that Max hadn't come this far, but it was possible, he supposed. He touched his hat brim, turned his horse, and rode back, now angling slightly east. He guessed he should

121

have stuck with Max's trail, but he'd thought he could save time this way.

He trotted his horse, aware the animal would not last the day if he did not. He traveled steadily, until he came to Heller's place. But instead of riding in, he circled it, looking for Max's trail.

He didn't find the trail of Max's horse. But he did find the trail of a man afoot. It was heading straight into the Heller ranch.

He followed it, frowning to himself. Max's horse must have taken a fall, he decided, and broken a leg doing it. Which had left Max afoot, with this the closest place at which he could get another horse.

Heller's place was deserted. His call brought no one to the door. He followed the trail to the corral, saw where Max had mounted, and picked up the trail of the horse, continuing east. Half a mile from the house, however, he found where the horse had stopped.

Max had hesitated here for a long, long time. There were many hoofprints, and a couple of cigarette stubs. Then the trail reversed itself.

He followed it, smiling grimly to himself. Max was sure as hell confused. And scared. He didn't have what it took to run away on his own. Or even to go back to his father's protection. He was apparently riding aimlessly—trying to make up his mind as to where he should go.

Mart kicked his horse into a lope, aware that the sun was sinking, that he had not many hours of daylight left. The miles fell steadily behind.

The sun was already down when he brought the Colfax place in sight. The trail detoured the house a mile to the north. Mart was famished and stared toward the house longingly. He'd had no breakfast and no noon meal. It was suppertime now.

But he did not turn aside. He continued along the trail. By the last rays of the setting sun, he caught sight of a horseman about a half mile ahead of him.

He spurred his lagging horse into a steady run. Light flamed on the clouds, turning the land to orange and gold. He began to gain on the horseman, who had not seen him yet.

And then, suddenly, he saw another horseman climb unexpectedly out of a wash a hundred yards in front of the first. He saw a puff of smoke. It seemed a long, long time before he heard the report.

The newcomer, recognizable even at this distance as an Indian, tumbled from the saddle. His horse galloped away.

The other horseman, who Mart could recognize as Max, rode to the man lying on the ground. Mart saw two more puffs of smoke, a moment later he heard the two reports.

He yanked out his revolver and fired three shots into the air. He yelled, but he knew how useless yelling was.

Max turned his head. He saw Mart and stared at him for a moment. Then he whirled his horse and sank his spurs.

Mart rode the remaining distance to the Indian lying on the ground. From a hundred yards, he recognized the man. It was Angry Bear.

He dismounted, and knelt at the old chief's side. He picked up the thin, wrinkled wrist and felt for pulse. None was detectable.

He stood up, staring down at the dead chief, cursing bitterly and helplessly. Damn a man who acted out of panic all the time! Angry Bear had constituted no threat to Max. He probably hadn't even seen Max until a moment before Max shot him out of his saddle. But what the devil had the old chief been doing here?

He glanced in the direction Max had gone, helpless fury raging in his mind. And suddenly he lunged for his horse, vaulted to the saddle, and rode toward the Indian's horse, which now stood a hundred yards away, grazing quietly.

He took down the rope from his saddle. From twenty-five feet, he made his throw.

The loop settled over the Indian pony's neck. Dismounting, Mart walked toward the trembling horse, hand-over-hand along the rope. Reaching the animal, he grasped the reins, then removed the loop. He mounted, reined around, and thundered after Max.

The horse ran well, and Mart knew he had a good chance of catching Max before it turned completely dark. Max's shape was dim in the darkening dusk, but Mart was gaining fast. Max's horse was as worn out as his own had been, but the Indian's horse was fairly fresh.

He was now only a quarter-mile from Max. Max turned his head and glanced over his shoulder. His face seemed very white in the fading light. He spurred his horse savagely but the animal was already running as fast as he could.

The distance between them closed to two hundred yards, to a hundred. Max yanked his revolver, turned in the saddle, and fired repeatedly at Mart, stopping only when the gun was empty. He began frantically trying to reload.

Mart shook out a loop in his rope. From a distance of twenty feet, he made his throw.

The loop settled over Max's head, slipped down around his chest, and tightened, pinning his arms to his sides. Mart passed the rope end around his body and yanked the Indian pony to a halt.

The rope snapped taut. Mart left the back of the Indian horse at the same time Max was yanked out of his saddle. The two hit the ground almost simultaneously.

Max's horse stopped immediately. The Indian pony continued to run, disappearing into the dusk.

Breath was partially knocked out of Mart, but he fought to his feet, gasping and choking for air. He stumbled toward Max, who still held his empty gun. Max threw it and Mart ducked. It missed him by a couple of feet.

He pulled back on the rope, again pinning Max's arms to his sides. Max came to his knees, and as Mart drew near, lunged at him.

Mart kicked furiously, filled with disgust and anger at what Max had done. His boot caught Max in the mouth, smashing his lips against his teeth, bringing blood, taking all the fight out of him. Mart said harshly, 'Get up, you son-of-a-bitch! You're going to jail.'

Max got up, and Mart pushed him roughly toward his horse. When they reached him, Mart mounted and turned back toward the place where the body lay, pulling Max along behind at the end of the rope. Max fell once, and Mart dallied the rope and dragged him for fifty feet. After that, Max stayed on his feet.

They reached the Indian's body. Here, Mart dropped the rope, then rode to catch the horse he had ridden here. He led the animal to the body, helped Max load it, then tied it down. He mounted again and, herding Max ahead, leading the horse on which the Indian's body lay, headed toward the Colfax house.

There were lamps burning in the kitchen. Marian came to the door and peered into the darkness. Mart called, 'It's me, Marian. I've got Max and the body of Angry Bear. I need fresh horses for the trip to town.'

He dismounted wearily and watched her approach. There would be hell to pay when he reached town. But there would be more hell to pay when the Cheyennes found out that Angry Bear was dead.

CHAPTER THIRTEEN

With wide eyes and white face, Marian stared at the body slung across the saddle of Mart's horse. Her voice was shocked and numb. 'What happened? How ...? He was alive an hour ago. He brought me home.'

'Brought you home? From where?'

'From the reservation.'

'What were you doing there?'

She glanced at Max, standing sullen and morose a dozen feet away. Then she said, 'I wanted to know, Mart. Can't you see, I *had* to know.'

'And Angry Bear came back with you so you'd be safe?'

She nodded wordlessly.

Mart felt almost sick at his stomach. He said, 'I'll catch some horses out of the corral. Come on, Max.'

Mart took Max's rope from the saddle and, leading the two horses, followed the man to the corral. Marian came along behind. Mart tossed the rope to Max and said harshly, 'Catch us three. And hurry up.'

One by one, Max brought horses to the corral gate. Mart changed the saddle from Max's horse to one of the fresh one's first. Then he lifted Angry Bear's body and laid it across the saddle. He tied it down.

He changed the saddle from his own horse to the second one Max brought. He took a third saddle from the top corral pole for the last horse.

Gathering up the reins of two of the horses, he mounted the third. He said harshly to Max, 'Mount up!'

Max mounted sullenly. Mart glanced down at Marian. 'You can't stay here. Angry Bear's horse got away from me, and he'll go home. In the morning, they'll trail him here and find out what happened. They'll kill you and burn the house.'

'Ed and Ben will be home soon.'

'Tell 'em to come on into town.'

She nodded wordlessly. She stared up at him for a moment, her face only a blur in the darkness. She said softly, 'Mart . . .'

'What?'

'Nothing. Nothing I guess.'

He said, 'Promise me. That you'll come into town even if Ben and Ed won't.'

'All right Mart.' Her voice was subdued and had a quality to it that was like a small girl's.

Mart turned and rode toward town. She'd

be all right out here tonight. There'd be no trouble yet. But if she hadn't come in by morning, he'd have to come out and bring her in.

With Mart leading two horses, it meant that Max was forced to ride side by side with the dead Indian. He stood it silently for about a half mile. Then, suddenly, he screeched, 'For Christ's sake, Mart! I can't ride all the way to town like this! What are you trying to do to me?'

Mart halted. He passed Max his reins. Then, taking the rope from the saddle, he dropped a loop over Max's body and tightened it. He said, 'Ride ahead then.'

Max forged ahead, and they continued on toward town.

It was late when they reached it. A couple of saloons were still open, but most of the town was dark.

Mart dismounted in front of the jail. Max went ahead of him without being told. Silently he went into one of the cells at the rear of the building. Mart slammed the door, locked it, and pocketed the key.

In the office, he lighted a lamp. He didn't know what to do with the body of Angry Bear. The Cheyennes would want it, would want to give it a ceremonial burial, he knew. Finally he went out and led the horse up the street to Doc's. He tied it and went up the walk to the door.

There was a lamp burning. He knocked softly.

The door opened. Doc peered out at him. 'He's better, Mart. He's breathing better and . . . well, he might make it after all.'

Mart nodded, relief running through him so strongly it made him weak. He remembered Angry Bear and said, 'I've got Angry Bear's body out here. It will have to go back to the reservation in the morning. Can I leave it here tonight?'

'Angry Bear? For Christ's sake, who killed him?'

Mart said wearily, 'Max. Who else? Can I leave him here?'

'Sure Mart. Bring him in. Where's Max now?'

'In jail. And about time, too.'

He went back out to the street, untied Angry Bear's body, and carried it into the house. He followed Doc to an unused room at the rear of the house and laid the Indian's body on a bed.

Doc whistled softly. 'There'll be hell to pay over this.'

Mart nodded.

'What are you going to do?'

Mart shrugged wearily. He looked helplessly at Doc. 'I don't know yet. I've got tonight to decide.'

'Burke's over at the hotel. He came in this evening after he heard Sam had been shot.'

Mart felt relief wash over him. He wasn't all alone. Burke couldn't help him with the sheriff's duties, but he might help in the matter of Angry Bear. He said, 'I'll go talk to him.'

He went out, mounted the horse on which he had brought in the body of Angry Bear, and rode to the hotel. He tied the horse and went inside.

The night clerk, Hal Lincoln, was reading a Cheyenne newspaper at the desk. He glanced up and Mart asked, 'What room is Elvin Burke in, Hal?'

'Six. But he's asleep, Mart. Can't it wait for morning?'

Mart shook his head. He turned, crossed the lobby, and climbed the stairs. He knocked on the door of number 6.

He heard the bed creak inside the room and heard Burke's sleepy voice, 'Who is it?'

'Mart Leathers, Mr. Burke. I've got to talk to you.'

The bed creaked again, and a moment later the bolt slid back. The door opened.

Burke was attired in his underwear. His hair was touseled. He said, 'Come on in. I'll light the lamp.'

He fumbled in his pants for a match and lighted the lamp. He pulled on the pants, then sat down heavily on the side of the bed.

Mart closed the door. 'Angry Bear is dead, Mr. Burke. Max murdered him.'

131

Burke stared at him in stunned silence. He licked his lips, then passed a hand over his face in a gesture of numb bewilderment. 'Why? For God's sake, what made him do a stupid thing like that?'

Mart pulled out a chair and straddled it, resting his arms on its back. He didn't answer Burke because he could see the agent didn't expect an answer from him. He said, 'The body has got to go out to the reservation in the morning. And then there'll be hell to pay.'

'You got Max in jail?'

Mart nodded.

Burke sat there silently for a moment, pale, frowning, a look that was almost panicky in his eyes. He said finally, 'I can't hold 'em back, Mart. Nobody can hold 'em back. I'd better get some troops in here.'

He reached for his shirt, stood up, and put it on. He sat down and put on his boots. He said, 'Let's get down to the telegraph office.'

He crammed on his hat and opened the door. Mart blew out the lamp and followed, closing the door behind him. The two silently went down the stairs, across the lobby, and out into the night.

Mart untied his horse and walked beside Burke, leading it. He picked up the other two horses at the jail and led all three down the street until he reached the livery barn. Here he said, 'You go on ahead, Mr. Burke. I'll catch up.'

He took the horses inside, unsaddled them, and then led them to the corral out back. He turned them in, and on the way back dropped the three bridles beside the saddles he had removed earlier. He went outside and down the street to the railroad station.

Burke had awakened Dan Lester, the telegraph operator. In trousers and underwear, Lester was lighting a lamp in the telegraph office. Burke grabbed a pad and pencil and began to write out his message to the commandant at Fort McKinney. When he had finished, he handed it to Dan, who read it swiftly. He glanced up at Burke when he had finished, his eyes scared. Without a word, he crossed to his instrument.

Burke said, 'If there's any reply, I'll be at the hotel.'

Lester nodded. His key clicked rapidly. Burke went out, and Mart followed. The Indian Agent stopped on the station platform and fished for a cigar. He bit off the end and lighted it. He glanced at Mart's face. 'Now what? Those troops won't get here in time. By this time tomorrow every Cheyenne on the reservation will be putting war paint on.'

'Maybe ... if I could get the circuit judge here right away ... if Max was tried and convicted ... maybe that would satisfy them.'

'It's worth a try.' But Burke's tone said that he was not convinced.

Mart turned and re-entered the telegraph

133

office. He wrote out his message on a blank and handed it to Dan when he had finished sending Burke's. Dan read this one too, nodded, and returned to the key. Mart said, 'Get his answer to me as soon as you get it, will you, Dan?'

'Sure, Mart.' Dan turned his head. 'How's Sam?'

'Better.'

He went back out. Burke's cigar made a glowing spot in the darkness. Mart asked, 'Want some coffee?'

Burke grunted assent and the two went up the street toward the jail. Mart built up the fire and put the coffee on. Burke sat in the sheriff's swivel chair, frowning, puffing occasionally on his cigar. Mart asked, 'Will you take Angry Bear's body back to the reservation tomorrow?'

'Sure. I was figuring on it. I'm about the only one who could do it and stay alive.'

'I ought to have an answer from the judge by then. You'll be able to tell 'em when the trial will be.'

The coffee filled the air with its aroma. Mart got two cups and poured them full. He took one to Burke, who sipped it appreciatively.

Mart rolled himself a cigarette. He began to wonder where the Colfax brothers were. He frowned slightly as he thought of Otto Gleason. Otto didn't yet know what his son had done.

He heard steps on the walk outside, and Dan Lester came in. He handed a yellow paper to Burke, another to Mart. Mart read his message swiftly. It said, 'Schedule trial Friday morning, 10 A.M.' It was signed, 'Austin Billings, judge.'

Two days from now, he thought. Two days to hold the lid on the situation here. He looked at Burke. 'I hope your news is better than mine.'

Burke said, 'They're coming. They're leaving the fort in the morning. But they can't get here until late Thursday or early Friday, no matter what they do.'

Dan Lester was waiting, looking from one to the other questioningly. Mart said, 'Thanks, Dan. All we can do now is wait.'

Lester nodded and went out. His footsteps on the boardwalk faded and died away. Burke stretched and got to his feet. 'I'd just as well go back to bed. But I doubt if I'll get much sleep.'

Mart walked to the door with him. He stood on the boardwalk outside and watched the Indian Agent walk toward the hotel.

He did not go in immediately. The air was cool, and there was a breeze from the southwest. He felt as though every nerve in his body was fiddlestring tight. Nervously he rolled another cigarette and puffed it until it burned his fingers. He threw it down and stepped on it. Then, with a fatalistic little shrug he went back into the office and blew out the lamp.

He laid down on the bunk and stared at the ceiling. How long, he wondered. How long?

Burke wouldn't get out there with the body until noon at the earliest. It would take the rest of tomorrow for riders that would be sent out from Angry Bear's village to reach the other villages. A council of chiefs would be called. That would take most of the following day. So it would be Friday before any action could be taken by the Cheyennes. Except, perhaps, for a few independent raids carried out by hotheaded young men without the knowledge or consent of their chiefs.

Otto Gleason and his crew would have to come into town. So would the Colfax brothers and Heller and Duer. They would be first attacked. But what if they wouldn't come?

He scowled fiercely in the darkness. Damn them, he couldn't *make* them come. If they wouldn't, they'd just have to take the consequences.

He closed his eyes and tried to sleep. He remembered suddenly that he'd had nothing at all to eat yesterday. No wonder he was so discouraged. No wonder he couldn't sleep.

He got up and began to pace back and forth, growing hungrier now because there was nothing he could do about his hunger until the hotel kitchen opened at five.

He saw the dawn come and saw the sun rise,

136

blood red, in the east. He watched the clock until the hands pointed to five o'clock. Then he locked the office door and headed for the hotel.

CHAPTER FOURTEEN

Hal Lincoln was snoring softly behind the desk, sprawled out in a leather-covered chair. The place was otherwise deserted.

Mart crossed the lobby, went through the deserted dining room, and opened one of the swinging doors that led to the kitchen. There was the smell of woodsmoke here and heat from the freshly kindled fire in the huge iron stove. A coffeepot was simmering on the front of it.

Pete Holley, the hotel cook, turned his head as Mart came in. 'You look like you'd been up all night.'

'I have. And I forgot to eat yesterday.' He sank down into a straight-backed chair, stretching his legs out in front of him.

'Want a steak?'

Mart nodded.

Pete left the kitchen and came back a few moments later with a steak and a handful of potatoes. He put a skillet on the stove and dumped some lard into it. He began to peel the potatoes. As he worked, he asked, 'How's

Sam?'

'Doc says he'll probably make it.'

'I hear you caught Max.'

Mart nodded.

'And I hear he killed some Injun.'

Mart grinned at him. 'You heard a lot, considering that I brought him to town in the middle of the night.'

Pete grinned. 'I came by the railroad depot. I talked to Dan.'

Mart stared at him sourly. He should have expected this, he supposed. Lester wasn't supposed to divulge the contents of the telegrams he sent or received, but that didn't prevent him from giving out general information he gleaned from the telegrams. Mart knew that by eight o'clock the news would be all over town.

The skillet was smoking. Pete dropped the steak into it, and the room began to fill with its delicious smell. Mart's mouth watered, and his stomach developed a sharp ache of hunger. Pete put some chopped-up potatoes in with the steak. He got a plate, a glass, and some silverware and carried them into the dining room. He placed them on the table nearest the door.

Mart got up, crossed to the stove, and inhaled the smell of the steak, licking his lips. Almost reluctantly he went into the dining room and sat down. A few minutes later Pete brought in a platter with the steak and

138

potatoes on it.

Mart ate ravenously. He gulped three cups of coffee and drank two glasses of milk. He couldn't remember when anything had tasted so good.

But once his preoccupation with his hunger had disappeared, other thoughts pushed into his mind. He was in for trouble from the town. It would terrify most of the townspeople to know that Angry Bear had been killed. It would further terrify them to know that Burke had sent for troops.

He finished the steak and potatoes and mopped the plate with a piece of bread. He put a quarter beside his plate, got up and stuck his head into the kitchen. 'Thanks, Pete.' He walked through the dining room and into the lobby, limping slightly because of soreness in his leg where Max had jabbed him with the pitchfork several days before.

Hal Lincoln was awake now, talking animatedly with two other men at the desk. They saw Mart and one of them yelled at him, but he pretended not to hear and went outside.

Down at the jail three men were sitting on the bench, waiting for him. He took time to roll a cigarette, then walked along the street.

One of the men was Toby Rosenthal, who ran the town's largest mercantile store. Another was Ivan Wortman, who owned one of the saloons. The third was Ev Thorp, a cattle trader who lived at the hotel.

The three stood up as Mart approached. The expressions of all were sober and concerned. Wortman said, 'We hear you got Max Gleason in the lock-up, Mart.'

Mart nodded.

Wortman hesitated several moments before he said, 'With Sam laid up . . . Don't you think you ought to have some help?'

Mart said, 'Maybe. Why?'

'Because Otto and the rest of them out there aren't going to take this lying down. Not a one of that bunch will stand for Max being tried for killing a Cheyenne. And if he's convicted . . .'

Mart said, 'Who did you have in mind?'

Wortman glanced at Thorp. 'Why Ev and me, I guess. We'd be willing to help. The way we look at it, if Max goes free, then nothing on earth will stop the Cheyennes. There'll be the worst damn blood bath this country's ever seen.'

Mart nodded. 'All right. I wouldn't mind a little help. One of you can start right now while I try and get a little sleep.'

He went into the office. The three talked among themselves for a moment, then two of them left. Wortman came inside.

Mart went over and stretched out on the couch. His eyelids were leaden. He closed his eyes. He could hear the sheriff's swivel chair creak as Wortman sat down in it.

140

He was grateful for their help. Later on today he'd need it too. Otto and his crew would be coming in, probably accompanied by the Colfax brothers, Clem Heller, and Joe Duer. They'd probably demand Max's release and might even try to break him out.

Weariness overcame him, and he went to sleep thinking that later on he would have to ride out to the Colfax place for Marian. If she had not already come to town.

The room grew hot as the day advanced. Mart tossed, sweating, on the leather-covered couch. He had a few brief, fleeting dreams, but when he awoke he could not remember them. He stared at Wortman, still sitting in Sam Farley's swivel chair, then swung his feet to the floor, and sat up.

Groggily he ran his fingers through his touseled, dampened hair. He grinned and asked, 'What time is it?'

'Almost noon.' Wortman was smoking a pipe. He was a broad, short man with thick black hair on the backs of his hands. A blue shadow showed on his clean-shaven jaws. His eyes were blue, sharp, and penetrating.

'Anything happen?'

'Burke hired a buckboard about eight and drove up to Doc's. The two of them loaded the Indian in the back and covered him with a blanket. Then Burke drove out of town.'

'Anything else?'

Wortman frowned. His eyes, though calm,

were troubled. 'The saloons have been filling up. Thorp came by a while ago. Said there was talk of lynching Max and taking the body out to the village on Horsetooth Creek.'

Mart rolled a smoke, licked the paper, and stuck it into his mouth. He should have expected the lynch talk, he supposed, but he had not. He asked, 'Otto show up yet?'

'Not yet. Maybe he hasn't gotten the word that Max is in jail.'

Mart crossed to the washstand. He dumped some water in the pan and washed. He lathered, stropped Farley's razor several times, then began to shave. Before he had finished Wortman said, 'Here they come, Mart.'

Mart cleaned the razor, wiped it carefully and put it back in its case. He dried his face with a towel, then turned and went to the door.

Otto Gleason sat in a buggy out front. He had several of his crewmen with him. One was in the buggy with him, the others mounted. Mart opened the door, and stepped out onto the walk.

Otto scowled at him. 'I hear you got Max in jail.'

Mart nodded.

'For killin' Angry Bear? Or for shootin' Sam?'

'Both.'

'Sam's all right, ain't he?'

'Doc says he'll probably live, if that's what

you mean. I wouldn't say he was all right.'

'It's the Injun, then. Hell, Max oughta get a medal for that.'

Mart didn't argue it with him. He asked wearily, 'What do you want, Mr. Gleason?'

'I want him out of there, that's what I want. I'll put up bail.'

'You can't have him. The judge will have to decide if he can get out on bail, and he won't get here until Thursday night or Friday.'

'You gettin' smart with me?'

Mart said evenly, 'I'm not getting smart but Max stays in jail. Until Friday, when he goes to trial.'

Otto's face reddened. Veins stood out on his forehead. He growled, 'You son-of-a-bitch, you got it in for Max because of what he done to that damn Colfax girl.'

Mart clenched his jaws against the angry outburst he wanted to release. He stood there silently for several moments until he could speak calmly. Then he said, 'I'd bring your outfit into town if I was you. When the Cheyennes find out what Max has done ...' He left the sentence dangling.

'To hell with the Cheyennes. Maybe it's time they was taught a thing or two.' The old man fumbled beside him a moment and turned. In his hands was a rifle, pointed straight at Mart Leathers' chest. He said, 'Taplow, go on in and get Max out. If this son-of-a-bitch moves, I'll put a hole in him.'

143

Taplow swung from his horse. He went behind Mart and started into the jail. He stopped suddenly. Wortman stood in the doorway, a double-barreled shotgun in his hands. Wortman said softly, 'Get back on your horse, Taplow.'

Taplow swung his head and looked at Otto helplessly. He backed slowly as Wortman came out of the jail and took a place at Mart's side. Wortman said softly, 'Otto, Mart might hesitate about shooting you, but I won't. Now get the hell out of here and don't come back.'

Otto glared at him furiously. For a moment, Mart thought he might use the rifle anyway, but he changed his mind. He turned his head and said to the man beside him, 'Drive on.'

The rig moved away, followed by the horsemen Gleason had brought to town with him. Taplow, looking relieved, mounted his horse and trailed after them. Up in front of one of the saloons, Otto's rig stopped. He was lifted out of it and carried into the saloon.

Mart grinned weakly at Wortman. 'Thanks. It's a good thing you were here.'

Wortman shrugged. He went back inside and Mart, after a last glance at Otto's men trooping into the saloon, followed him.

There were three groups now, he thought. The first was composed of Wortman, Rosenthal, and Thorp, who were on the side of the law. There was another group of frightened townspeople who wanted to pacify

144

the Indians by lynching Max. And there were the ranchers, led by Otto Gleason, who wanted to break Max out of jail.

He said, 'I'm going up to that saloon and talk to them.'

'It won't do any good.'

'Maybe not. But Otto ought to be thinking about his place out there. It's the first one the Cheyennes will hit.'

Wortman nodded, and Mart went out. He walked slowly up the sunwashed street toward the saloon where Otto and his men had disappeared.

The day was warm and bright. He thought of Burke, driving out to the village on Horsetooth Creek with the body of Angry Bear. Burke was the Indian Agent. They knew and trusted him. But he was still taking an awful chance. Angry Bear's young men were hotheaded and aroused. They might shoot first, before Burke even got a chance to explain.

He reached the saloon and went inside. There was a growing worry in him about Marian, who might be all alone. Her brothers were gone most of the time. From midafternoon on, anything could happen out there. At Otto's place, at the Colfax place, or at Heller's. They were closest to the reservation.

Otto had been carried to a table in the corner of the saloon. His men were grouped

145

around him. Mart crossed the room and looked down at the embittered old man. 'I don't suppose you'll take advice from me, but I'd get back home if I was you. Burke isn't going to be able to hold back Angry Bear's young bucks. Your place is the first one they'll raid.'

Otto scowled at him. 'You're right about one thing. I won't take advice from you. But I left enough men to drive 'em off.'

'How many, Otto? How many will it take to drive the Cheyennes off?'

'I left four.'

'And Della?'

Otto glared. But he didn't reply. It was plain to Mart that Otto had planned to get back home before the Cheyennes arrived, but he had intended to get Max out of jail first.

He turned and left the saloon, not missing the glances of another group at one end of the bar.

Walking down the street toward the jail, he thought of Marian again. Desperately he wanted to leave town, but he knew he couldn't yet. Otto Gleason was probably going to attempt to break into the jail.

He'd just have to wait—until Otto had made his play. He couldn't afford to lose Max, no matter what.

Marian's brothers might still bring her in. There was a little time. But it was swiftly running out, like the sand in an hourglass.

CHAPTER FIFTEEN

Elvin Burke reached the village on Horsetooth Creek in midafternoon. Usually, at this time of day, the Cheyenne villages looked drowsy and half deserted, but such was not the case today. And, as he drove the buckboard into the village, Burke immediately saw why.

A riderless horse was the center of attention. Men, young and old, were gathered around it. Beyond the circle of men, a group of women and children chattered excitedly.

Burke breathed a long, slow sigh of relief. Angry Bear's horse had not come straight home. He had poked along, probably grazing as he came in the long, rich grass of the disputed ten-mile strip. He had obviously just now arrived.

Burke drove to the edge of the group, and it parted to let him through. He got down from the buckboard and peeled the blanket back.

A shocked murmur went up from the assembled Cheyennes. Burke yelled, 'Angry Bear is dead. He was killed by a white man. The white man who killed him is now in jail awaiting trial!'

The murmur grew dangerously. Here and there one of the young men shouted, crying out for revenge. Burke roared, 'You will have no revenge! That is not the white man's way!

The law will punish his killer.'

He shouted down, and the last of his words were lost. A group of young men was already forming at the edge of the milling group. Burke shouted, 'I have sent for troops. If you act foolishly now, you will answer to the cavalry.' He turned pleadingly to one of the medicine men. 'Stop them, Crippled Wolf. Stop them as Angry Bear would have done.'

The medicine man stared at him with impassive, opaque eyes. His mouth was a thin, hard line. He said, 'Angry Bear is dead.'

Burke felt his own anger rise. Why wouldn't they see? Why wouldn't they realize that their own violence would only add to the fires. He said, 'I told you his killer was in jail. I told you he would be punished for his crime.'

'Like those who burned our lodges were punished?'

The group of young men, eighteen or twenty strong, suddenly began to disperse. They would put on war paint and get their weapons. They would go to the horse herd beyond the village and catch mounts for themselves. Then they would leave.

Burke said, 'Crippled Wolf . . .' He stopped. Nothing he could say would change what was happening. The Cheyennes had been lied to and cheated in almost every dealing they ever had with the white men. They believed it would be no different now. Angry Bear might have restrained them, but Angry Bear was dead.

He climbed to the buckboard seat. He slapped the backs of the team with the reins and turned the rig around. He headed back toward Medicine Lodge instead of toward the Agency. All he could do now was warn the town and hope the troops arrived in time.

At sundown, Della Chavez drew a bucket of water from the pump and carried it around to the front of the house. She poured it carefully into a network of shallow ditches that irrigated her flower bed. It still looked a mess, she thought, from those two big lummoxes rolling in it, fighting.

She returned to the pump for a second bucket and poured it similarly on the flower bed. Then she straightened and looked at the land around the ranch.

She saw them coming at almost the same instant she heard their shrill, yipping cries. Out in the open space between bunkhouse and house a man yelled hoarsely, 'Della! Get inside!'

She stared at the oncoming Indians unbelievingly. Then, as though suddenly realizing they were real and not some fantasy of her mind, she dropped the bucket and scurried for the house. She went in, slammed, and locked the door. Hurriedly, she ran to the other door and locked it too. Outside a rifle roared, and another, and suddenly it was bedlam out there, with Indians screeching and

149

guns roaring like a string of giant firecrackers.

A horse nickered shrilly. Della ran to the window in time to see the animal fall, dumping his Indian rider less than a dozen yards from the front porch. The brave got up and ran but a rifle bullet brought him crashing down, to lie completely still. Della could see his face, a young face that was pale in death. She knew he could not be more than sixteen years old.

The sun had gone down and dusk crept grayly across the land. The Indians galloped away to halt their horses about three hundred yards from the house. They talked among themselves as though discussing their strategy.

The guns were silent. She could not see the men in the yard and knew they had concealed themselves. She wondered what would happen now. She waited, and the light continued to fade until at last she could not see the Indians any more.

A man knocked on the back door. Della called, 'Who is it?'

'It's Frank Valenti, Ma'am. They're gone. We'll keep watch, but I don't think we'll see 'em again until mornin'.'

Della did not reply. Valenti said, 'Lane's going to town to get Otto. Don't you worry, ma'am.'

She called, 'Thank you.'

Valenti said, 'Keep the door locked, though.'

'Yes.' She sat down nervously in one of the

straight-backed chairs to wait.

* * *

Mart reached the jail and went inside. Turning, he locked the door. He crossed the room to the gun-rack and took down two double-barreled shotguns. From a drawer he took a handful of shells and loaded them. He crossed the room to Wortman and handed one of the guns to him. Wortman grinned humorlessly. 'I take it you didn't change Otto's mind.'

Mart shook his head. 'He'll have to try. But it's going to have to be soon. He knows his place will be the first one they'll hit.'

Out back, Max began to yell. Mart went to the door and opened it. Max stood at his cell door, holding onto the bars. He said, 'Christ, don't I get anything to eat around here?'

Mart stared at him ruefully. 'I guess I forgot. I'll send out for something right away.'

He returned to the office. It had been so long since they'd had anyone in jail, he just wasn't used to providing for prisoners. He said, 'Max wants something to eat. I guess I forgot him this morning. Will you go up to the hotel and have something sent down?'

'Sure.' Wortman got up and laid the shotgun on the desk. Mart said, 'Take that along. And if you see Thorp, bring him back with you.'

Wortman picked up the shotgun and crossed to the door. He went out and Mart

151

locked the door behind him. Through the window he watched Wortman walk along the street and disappear into the hotel. He studied the street, seeing none of Otto's men. He went back to the chair and sat down.

Five minutes passed. Mart heard the wheels of a buggy in the street and got to his feet as Otto Gleason pulled his rig to a halt in front. Gleason let go instantly with a shotgun blast that shattered the window on the right side of the door. He bawled, 'Send him out, Mart! I got men all around this place.'

Mart, who had ducked behind the desk as the shotgun roared, shouted, 'Come and get him Otto! But I've got a shotgun too. First man through the door gets blown in two!'

He heard the screeching rasp of a file out back. Otto was supposed to hold him here, he guessed, while someone else filed Max's bars and got him out.

He wriggled toward the door leading to the cells, staying low. Otto let go another blast, and this one shattered the other window. Shot rattled against the roll-top desk.

Mart flattened himself on the floor and crawled back behind the desk. He poked his head around it and saw Otto calmly reloading his gun.

Damn the man anyway! He knew Mart wouldn't shoot him. He was as safe as he would be in bed at home. He also knew Mart wouldn't risk making a rush for the rear of the jail.

Otto released a third blast. This one tore the remaining jagged shards out of the window and rattled against the rear wall. Mart's anger began to stir. Damn them, they weren't going to get Max out!

He tensed for a rush to the rear door. He'd wait until Otto loosed his other barrel and then he'd made a run for it. Max might have a gun by now, but if Max tried to use it he'd cut his prisoner in two.

Otto seemed in no hurry to shoot again. Mart reached around the desk and got his hand on the brass cuspidor. He heaved it across the room.

Instantly Otto let go. Before the sounds of the shot tearing into the walls had died away, Mart was on his feet, running toward the door leading to the cells.

He slammed it open and leaped through, shotgun ready, hammer back. He kicked the door shut behind him.

Max had a gun all right. He started to raise it, then he stopped, his eyes fixed on the gaping twin bores of Mart's shotgun. Mart said, 'Drop it, you son-of-a-bitch!'

The gun clattered to the floor. Mart swung the shotgun toward the window where Taplow was filing at the bars from the outside. He said, 'It didn't work, Taplow. Drop the file and get the hell out of here.'

Taplow's face disappeared. Mart said, 'Kick

153

the gun out in the corridor, Max.'

Max kicked the revolver along the floor. It slid to the bars and stopped. Mart crossed to it, knelt and picked it up, keeping the shotgun pointed at Max and not taking his eyes off the man. He straightened, stuffing the revolver into his belt.

He returned to the door cautiously and opened it enough to look through. Otto's buggy was still out front, but Otto no longer had a gun. Wortman stood on one side of it, Thorp on the other. Gleason's face was almost purple with his rage.

Mart crossed the office, unlocked the shattered door, and stepped outside. He said, 'Let him go.'

Wortman and Thorp stepped back. Gleason picked up the reins and slapped the buggy horse with them. The horse trotted down the street. From behind the jail came Otto's riders. They fell in behind the rig without looking back.

Mart glanced up the street and saw Pete Holley approaching, carrying a tray. He took it from Pete, who was staring, openmouthed, at the destruction Otto's shotgun had caused. He carried it inside.

He unlocked Max's cell door and put the tray on the floor. He backed out and re-locked the door. He returned to the office and stared ruefully at the glass-littered floor. He reached automatically for the broom.

His hands were shaking, and he gripped the broom more tightly so it wouldn't show. That had been a close one. Too close.

Otto probably wouldn't try again. He was going to be too busy defending his ranch against the Cheyennes. But Wortman had said there was another group in town—a group that was talking of a lynch party for Max. He'd have to get the windows replaced and the door repaired before tonight.

As though understanding his thoughts, Wortman asked, 'Want me to get Dave Miller down here to replace that broken glass?'

Mart nodded. He hesitated a moment, then asked, 'Think you and Thorp could hold things down the rest of the afternoon? I ought to go out to the Colfax place. Marian Colfax was supposed to come in to town but she hasn't shown up yet.'

'Sure Mart. I doubt if there'll be any more trouble here. At least until dark.'

Wortman headed diagonally across the street toward Dave Miller's house. Mart walked toward the stable to get a horse. A group of people across the street was staring at the sheriff's office curiously.

Mart suddenly remembered that he had returned his own horse to the small stable behind his house a couple of days before. He cut diagonally across a vacant lot and headed for the place.

The horse was in the small corral, his

muzzle in the watering trough. Mart caught him and saddled him. He started out of town, then turned, and rode back to Doc Williams' house. He dismounted, tied the horse and went up the walk.

The door was open. He called, 'Doc?'

'Yeah. Come on in. Sam wants to talk to you.'

Mart went in. Doc beckoned from a room opening off the parlor and Mart went into it.

Sam glanced at him weakly from the bed. Mart crossed to it and looked down. The change in Sam was frightening. Mart grinned. 'How are you, Sam?'

The sheriff nodded weakly, but he did not speak immediately. When he did, his voice was like a croak. 'Doc says you're doin' a damn good job.'

Mart's grin widened. He'd needed someone to say that right now. Sam croaked, 'Keep it up.'

Mart nodded, his throat tight. He turned and left the room. He mounted and headed northeast out of town, toward the Colfax place. He saw Otto Gleason's buggy ahead and to his left a couple of miles away. Otto's men were spread out in a line behind it.

He kicked his horse into a lope.

CHAPTER SIXTEEN

Mart's horse was fresh, and for a while after leaving town he let the animal choose his own pace, let him run off his high spirits. After that he held the horse to a steady trot.

Gleason and his men were soon out of sight. Mart traveled steadily toward the Colfax place. The sun sank toward the western horizon. It was hanging like a brass ball half above and half below the horizon when he heard the first shots directly ahead of him.

Instantly he halted and held his horse very still. He listened. The shots came with spasmodic irregularity and when he realized that, he breathed a long, slow sigh of relief, because it told him the Colfax brothers were alive, holed up someplace and fighting back.

He was still nearly a mile away and there was not much cover between here and the house because the land was mostly flat. He could see the grove of trees that surrounded the ranch buildings. He urged his horse into motion again and rode straight toward the trees.

From half a mile away, from the crest of a low rise, he could see the house plainly. He could even see, in the orange rays of the setting sun, the little puffs of smoke coming from the upstairs windows of the house.

He sat there motionless for several minutes, making mental note of the location of every answering puff of smoke in the yard facing the house. Then, suddenly, he raked his horse's sides with his spurs.

The startled animal leaped ahead. They probably wouldn't see him until he was almost upon them, he thought. For an instant afterward, they would think he was one of several. He intended to encourage that illusion by shooting as swiftly as he could.

Rapidly the distance between him and the house decreased. And then, suddenly, he saw half a dozen young Indian braves leap from their hiding places and point their guns at him.

He fired, holding his point of aim low. He heard one of them howl and saw him tumble to the ground.

The house loomed up immediately before him. He kept the horse headed straight at the kitchen door as though he would ride through.

He was now the focal point of all their shooting. But from the upstairs windows, Ed and Ben Colfax were also shooting with spaced regularity at targets Mart's coming had exposed.

Mart tensed to dismount, timing it so that he would hit the ground less than a dozen yards from the door. In the few moments it took him to reach the door from that position, he would be shielded by the body of the horse.

He saw the door open slightly, saw Marian's

white face in the opening. He started to leave his horse . . .

Suddenly the horse's forelegs buckled. His head went down. Mart was flung violently over the horse's head, directly toward the partly opened door.

He struck it with his shoulders. It slammed open violently and Mart skidded through, halfway across the kitchen floor.

Marian, who had stepped aside when she saw him coming, now hurried toward him, an expression of horror on her face. Mart lay on his back gasping for several moments. Then he raised his head and stared at the doorway, partially blocked by his kicking horse. He crawled to the horse and yanked his rifle from the saddle boot. He levered a shell into it and rested it on the horse's side.

He could see the bodies of two Indians. He could see a third, crawling painfully toward the cover of a shed. He heard a shot upstairs and saw dust kick up six inches from the crawling brave.

He turned his head and looked at Marian. 'You all right?'

She nodded. Mart's leg was hurting fiercely where Max Gleason had struck him with the pitchfork tine. There were two or three skinned places on him that burned. The horse kicked helplessly several times and then lay still.

Mart said, 'I thought you were going to

159

come to town.'

'I couldn't get Ben and Ed to come. They said the minute they left the Cheyennes would burn the place.'

Mart nodded. He stared at the yard outside. He saw no movement now. The crawling Indian had disappeared.

The light was fading rapidly. Soon it would be dark. The Indians would pull back to wait for dawn.

A moment later, Ben Colfax entered the room. 'Did you get Max to jail all right?'

Mart nodded.

Ben grinned faintly. 'And I guess you got the body of Angry Bear back to the Cheyennes. What the hell do they think, that we killed him?'

Mart shook his head. 'Burke took the body back. I suppose he told 'em Max did it and that Max was in jail. But you know how Indians think. When they want revenge against a white man, any white man will do.'

'Yeah. I know.' Ben stared at him for a moment. 'Mart . . . Will you take Marian into town?'

'That's what I came out here for.'

Ben went to the door and looked out into the yard. 'The horses are in the corral but I figure as soon as it gets dark enough, those bucks may try to turn 'em out. We'd better get over there now.'

He turned his head and yelled, 'Ed! We're

160

goin' to the corral after horses. Keep us covered from up there.'

He jumped over the body of Mart's horse and sprinted across the yard. Gun in hand, Mart followed him.

Half a dozen shots racketed. Instantly Ed opened up from the upstairs window of the house. He was firing at the flashes, and he scored at least one hit because Mart heard a high yell of pain. The shooting stopped, whether because of fear of Ed's accuracy or because they could no longer see to shoot, Mart didn't know.

Ben went into the corral and took down a rope from one of the poles. He said, 'Just cover me from the gate, Mart. I'll get a couple of horses.'

'What about the others?'

'We won't need 'em. We'll either hold this place or we won't. We ain't going to run away.'

He roped out a horse and led it to the gate. Mart bridled it, then waited until Ben caught a second one. Leading the two horses, they crossed the yard to the tackroom in the front end of the barn. Here they saddled both animals.

Mart stared out the door into the night. The only sound was the faint stirring of the wind in the eaves of the barn, the rustling of the trees beyond the yard on the other side of the corral. Ben came up beside him and whispered, 'Think you can get through?'

'We'll get through. Go get Marian and bring her here. We can get mounted right here in the barn and be going at a run by the time we clear the doors. By the time they realize what's going on, we'll be in the clear.'

'Why couldn't Ed and me drive those loose horses out of the corral first? They'd throw 'em off.'

Mart said, 'It'd throw Marian too. If she thought you two were out here alone without horses, she wouldn't even go to town. I'd have to drag her in by force.'

'Guess you're right. All right. I'll go get Marian. I'll leave Ed to cover from the upstairs window.'

Mart stood at the side of the door. He watched Ben cross the yard toward the house. Ben disappeared in the darkness before he was halfway there.

Mart waited impatiently. He kept glancing toward where he knew the Indians were and thinking if they weren't so damned superstitious about fighting at night, he'd be dead right now. So would Ben and Ed. So would Marian.

Tomorrow was Thursday. Troops ought to be arriving sometime late tomorrow. Maybe Ben and Ed could hold out until help came. Or maybe they could make it so damned expensive that the young braves would give up and leave.

He heard a flurry of movement from the

direction of the house. An instant later, Ben came into the barn with Marian. Mart said, 'Get mounted, Marian. Hurry.'

She went toward the horses. Ben whispered softly, 'Gleason's place is on fire, Mart. I could see the glow in the sky.'

'Marian see it?'

'Huh uh. It ain't too plain just yet. Don't you let her turn around and come back, Mart, no matter what. Not even if you see things burning here. You understand?'

'Sure.' He swung to the back of the other horse and said sharply, 'Hold on, Marian!' As he said it, he gave her horse a savage cut across the rump with a short length of rope he'd picked up.

Her horse seemed to leap through the open barn doors. Mart was close behind, hitting her horse's rump at about every third jump. As they cleared the yard and started through the trees, he loosed a high, shrill yell and fired his revolver several times.

Then they were in the open, leaning low, riding as though the devil was close behind.

Mart glanced toward the Gleason place. The glow was plain now, and easily seen from here. Behind them, guns were flashing in the upstairs window of the Colfax house, in the barn door, and in the grove of trees. Mart did not slacken his pace. He surged up abreast of Marian's horse and held this position.

They had gone almost a mile before she saw

the glow of Gleason's burning ranch. Her face made a pale blur in the darkness. Mart heard her breath sigh out softly. He said, 'Don't worry. Your brothers are going to be all right.'

'Gleason's place is on fire. And they've got nearly a dozen men.'

'Sure. The Cheyennes are trying harder for Gleason's place than they ever will for yours. Gleason's men burned their lodges the other night, and Max killed Angry Bear.'

'I hope . . . Mart, I want to go back. I'm not going to leave Ben and Ed alone.'

He reached over and grabbed the reins out of her hand. She struggled briefly, but it was no use. Mart got the reins and dragged her horse along close behind his. He said, 'You're not going back. I'll send them some help as soon as the troops arrive.'

'Mart, please!'

'They'll do better if they don't have to worry about you.'

That was true at least, he thought, even if his statement that her brothers would be all right was not. Two men couldn't keep the Indians from setting fires. And once things started burning . . . the Indians could stay back out of the firelight and shoot at everything that moved. But there was nothing he could do about it. Ben and Ed had made their choice. He couldn't force them to abandon their home.

He thought of Max Gleason and cursed

164

mildly to himself. One man could stir up a hell of a lot of trouble once he got started at it.

Marian was silent all the way to town. He didn't know for sure, but he supposed she was thinking of her mother, who had been kidnaped during an earlier uprising.

For himself, he was wondering how bad this uprising was going to get. The Cheyennes on the reservation could destroy every town north of Fort McKinney before enough force could be mobilized to stop them. They could burn every ranch within a hundred miles. Even if troops arrived tomorrow, it would be too late.

As he entered town, he faced one fact in his mind. He couldn't stop an uprising if there was to be one. He couldn't prevent the Indians from burning and looting. He couldn't even be sure of Max Gleason's conviction on the charge of murdering Angry Bear.

There were three things he could do, and they were the same things Sam Farley would have done had he been in charge. He could hold Max Gleason for trial. He could see to it that he went to trial. And he could carry out the sentence of the court.

These were his individual responsibilities, his part in preventing the spread of violence and death.

CHAPTER SEVENTEEN

There was a deceptive quiet about the town when Mart rode into it. He realized immediately that the townspeople had not received the word. They didn't know Gleason's place had been burned or that the Colfaxes had been attacked. But now that Marian was here, it would be impossible to conceal what was happening.

He rode straight to the hotel, dismounted, and helped Marian to the ground. Her face was pale, her eyes worried. He said, 'Ben and Ed can take care of themselves, Marian.'

She smiled and nodded uncertainly. He stared at her worriedly for a moment. At last she said, 'If you're worrying about me leaving town and going back ... well, you don't need to, Mart. I'm not going to be foolish. I know both Ben and Ed want me to be here.'

He nodded, relieved. He said, 'I haven't eaten since breakfast. Give me ten minutes to check the jail. Then I'll meet you here and we'll eat. All right?'

She nodded and went inside. Mart led the two horses down the street to the jail.

Thorp was inside, his feet up on the desk. Mart asked, 'Everything all right?'

Thorp nodded. 'There's been some talk, but so far it's only talk.'

'What kind of talk?'

'That the only way to prevent an uprising is to lynch Max and deliver his body to the village on Horsetooth Creek.'

Mart nodded. 'Where's that bunch now?'

Thorp said, 'They were in Mike Androvich's place earlier. I think they all went over to the Silver Dollar.' He grinned wryly. 'Takes liquor to keep lynch talk going. You know that.'

Mart said, 'I'm going to eat. Lock the door when I leave and keep a shotgun handy.'

'Why? You think they might get drunk enough to be dangerous?'

Mart shook his head. 'I think they might get scared enough. I just brought Marian into town. Gleason's place is afire and the Colfax place is under attack.'

Thorp's feet hit the floor. He crossed the room to the gunrack and took a double-barreled ten-gauge down. He loaded it, then crossed the room, and locked the door after Mart. Mart went up the street toward the hotel. He probably should have cautioned Marian against talking about what was happening, but it wouldn't have done any good in the long run. Gleason or some of Gleason's men would be hitting town before very long. The town would know everything as soon as they did.

Marian was waiting for him inside the lobby of the hotel. There was a mixed group around her, questioning her excitedly. Mart interrupted, 'Nothing to get excited about. Troops will be here late tomorrow. So far, all we're sure about is that a few young men from the village on Horsetooth Creek are attacking Gleason's and the Colfaxes' ranch. Go on home and go to bed. The troops are on the way.'

He got hold of Marian's arm and led her into the dining room. He found a table near the front, beside a window through which he could watch the street. He watched several men leave the hotel and hurry toward the saloons. He said, 'There they go. In half an hour everybody in town will know.'

'I'm sorry, Mart. I shouldn't have said anything.'

'It doesn't matter. Gleason or some of his men will be in before the night is over. The town's got to know sooner or later.'

'What's going to happen, Mart? Will it be like . . . ?'

'Like twenty years ago? I doubt it.' He studied her closely for a moment, then changed the subject suddenly. 'Maybe this isn't the time, and I know it's not the place. But I want to tell you something. I love you, and I want to marry you.' His face felt hot.

For a moment Marian did not reply. Her glance was very soft as it rested on Mart's face.

Mart suddenly had a feeling she was going to say no. He said quickly, 'You don't have to say anything right now. You don't have to

168

make up your mind. But if you're thinking about the chance that you've got some Indian blood . . . you can forget it. It doesn't matter to me, one way or the other. I just plain don't care.'

Her eyes misted slightly as she continued to smile at him. The waitress came to the table and said, 'Evening, Miss Colfax. Hello, Mart.'

He nodded, watching Marian's face as she ordered supper. He ordered, and the waitress left. Glancing out the window, he saw a group down in front of the Silver Dollar. They seemed to be arguing.

He watched them worriedly until the waitress brought their meals. His attention was distracted for a minute or two. When he looked out the window again, the group was gone.

He ate quickly, hungrily. A strange feeling of uneasiness was growing in him now. He hadn't liked the way that group in front of the Silver Dollar had disappeared.

Marian said, 'Something's the matter. What is it, Mart?'

'Thorp said there'd been some lynch talk in town. I guess I'm just nervous.' He smiled apologetically at her. 'Don't let me spoil your meal.'

She said, 'You're finished with yours. Would you like to go? You don't have to stay just to be polite.'

'Would you mind? I'll come back as soon as

169

I make sure everything's all right.'

He got up, smiled at her, then hurried from the room. The feeling of urgency in him increased. He strode across the lobby and out into the night.

He stood for a moment, staring down the street in the direction of the jail. The street was virtually deserted now. The town seemed peaceful, even sleepy.

In spite of appearances, the nervousness in Mart increased. Suddenly he stepped off the hotel veranda and began to hurry toward the jail. Before he had gone ten steps, he increased his pace to a steady trot.

He glanced to right and left, searching vacant lots, searching the dark passages between buildings with his eyes. Still he had heard nothing—seen nothing to account for his feeling that . . .

He frowned to himself as he broke into a run. And then, suddenly from his right and ahead of him, he heard a shout.

He snatched out his gun and thumbed the hammer back as men streamed out of a vacant lot to block the boardwalk in front of him. He halted and stood spread-legged in the semidarkness, waiting.

A man yelled, 'We're going to take him, Mart. We don't want to hurt nobody, but we're going to take him and give him to the Cheyennes. It's the only thing that's going to keep them from going on a worse rampage.'

Mart didn't reply. He was still a good hundred yards from the jail. If he could reach it, he and Thorp could probably hold them off. But he didn't see how he was going to reach it. Not with this bunch blocking the way. They were scared enough to be unpredictable.

He shrugged resignedly. 'All right. There ain't much I can do to stop you, I guess.'

'That's the smart way to talk, Mart. Max ain't worth getting killed over the way we look at it.'

Mart turned, holstering his gun as he did. He walked back toward the hotel. He heard a murmur of talk behind him as several of them questioned his giving up so easily.

He kept walking, trying not to hurry noticeably. In a moment they'd realize that he didn't intend to give up. They'd come after him, intent on disarming him and making him a prisoner until after they had succeeded in forcing the jail.

He heard a shout, 'Get him! He ain't givin' up!' He heard the sudden pound of running feet on the boardwalk behind him.

He broke into a run, and ducked into the first dark passageway that showed itself beside him. He sprinted along it, gun in hand, glancing over his shoulder as he did.

He came to the end of it, where tin cans and trash were piled two feet high. Too late, he tried to jump. He tripped and came crashing to the ground.

Guns exploded at the other end of the passageway. Bullets struck the pile of cans and ricocheted away into the night. Mart rolled frantically to one side.

Gaining the protection of the building corner, he got to his feet and ran again. He could hear them pounding along the passageway after him. Some of them jumped over the pile of cans. Some did not. He grinned as he heard them thrashing around, cursing drunkenly.

He reached the alley and pounded along it, running as hard as he could. He cut across a vacant lot and headed directly toward the jail. The bunch of them burst out of the alley into the vacant lot behind him, and immediately an angry shout went up.

Mart reached the jail wall. He was in shadow now, he knew, and probably not visible to them. Quickly he ran to the front of the building.

There were still a few pieces of glass lying around. They crunched beneath Mart's booted feet. He tapped on the door, and Thorp opened it. Mart said, 'Lock the door and blow out the lamp.'

He crossed the room hurriedly and got a shotgun from the rack. The room went dark as Thorp blew out the lamp.

The air was strong with the smell of putty used to replace the window glass. Mart opened the door leading to the cells and called. 'You

172

all right, Max?'

'Sure. I'm all right. What's going on?'

'Get over in the corner of your cell and keep your mouth shut. Stay there, no matter what happens. There's a bunch outside that wants to deliver you to the Cheyennes. I don't think they care whether they deliver you alive or dead.'

Max did not reply, but Mart heard him stir and cross his cell.

Leaving the door ajar, he returned to the office. He could see them out front in the street, faceless, nameless, uncertain. He wondered how long it would be before they talked up enough courage to attack the jail.

Thorp asked softly, 'Now what? You think they'll try and take Max away from us?'

'I don't know. We'll just have to wait and see.'

'What if they do try? You ain't going to shoot into them, are you?'

Mart turned his head and looked at Thorp. 'Hell yes, I am.'

'Why don't you tell 'em that?'

'Maybe I will.' He crossed to the door, unlocked, and opened it. But he didn't yell at the men in the street. Because he heard something . . . It was the sullen thunder of hoofs coming from the north.

Indians? He had a sinking feeling in the pit of his stomach. Then he shook his head angrily. Hell, it couldn't be Indians. Not yet.

Not this soon. It had to be Gleason and his men.

They loomed up in the darkness, and he felt the sudden weakness of relief. The men were white. They could only be Otto's men. He yelled, 'Hold it! I want to talk to you!'

They hauled their horses to a halt in front of the jail. The townsmen had retreated across the street. Mart yelled, 'Where's Otto?'

'Comin'.' It was Joe Taplow's voice. For once it was subdued. Mart said, 'I saw fire up your way. How bad was it?'

'The whole damn works, house, barn, bunkhouse—everything.' There was considerable bitterness in Taplow's voice.

'Anybody killed?'

'Bob Higgins. Valenti's got a bullet in his arm. He's in the buggy with Otto. They oughta be here soon.'

The men across the street were coming forward now. Mart yelled, 'The whole bunch of you had better get together and plan some kind of defense for the town. Quit worrying about Max.'

Otto Gleason's buggy rattled past, with Otto driving it. Mart could see a lumped shape beside him, and there was a saddle horse tied on behind. A man lay across the horse's saddle, limp and still. The buggy went past without stopping and continued up the street to Doc Williams' house. Gleason's riders fell behind and followed it.

174

The mob across the street moved uptown. Someone was yelling at them and while Mart did not catch all the words, he caught enough to know one of their number was trying to organize them.

He backed into the sheriff's office and closed the door. He yelled at Max, 'You can quit worrying, Max. They've gone.'

He lighted the lamp and sat down wearily on the office couch. He stared at Thorp. He wondered if the troops would arrive in time, wondered if they'd reach Medicine Lodge before the Cheyennes did.

CHAPTER EIGHTEEN

Mart did not stay in the office long. Danger from the group that had wanted to lynch Max Gleason was past—for the time being at least. Otto and his crew constituted no immediate threat. They'd taken too bad a beating at the hands of the Indians to be worrying about breaking Max out of jail.

He got up and went to the door, saying, 'I'll be back soon.' Thorp nodded, and he went outside.

He stood for several moments on the walk. Gleason had started this, he thought, because of a single steer that had been found with an arrow in its side.

Shaking his head thoughtfully, he started up the street toward the hotel. More had actually been involved, he supposed, than a single steer. The real animosity had not been over that but over the new survey, over the ten-mile strip of grazing land that had been given back to the Cheyennes.

Furthermore, Otto Gleason had succeeded. He had accomplished his purpose. He'd made the Indians resort to violence.

He saw the buggy halted in front of Doc Williams' house. He saw the saddle horses of Gleason's crewmen tied along the fence. They were subdued and peaceful now, he thought, because they were exhausted and because one of them had been killed. But by tomorrow . . . Otto Gleason wasn't going to change. He still wasn't going to let Max be convicted and hanged if he could prevent it.

Furthermore, if the Indians attacked the town—tonight or tomorrow or at any time before the trial—then the chance that Max would be convicted would be gone. He'd be acquitted and released.

Mart found Marian on the hotel veranda, her eyes fixed on the buggy in front of Doc Williams' house and on the saddle horses tied to the fence. When she saw Mart she asked, 'What happened out at Gleason's, Mart?'

'Bob Higgins was killed. Frank Valenti got a bullet in his arm. Gleason's place was burned.'

Marian's face was pale. 'I'm worried about

176

Ben and Ed. Isn't there anything . . . ?' She stood up nervously.

'I'll see if I can get some men together and go out there. The Indians aren't going to attack again until dawn so they're all right until then.' He started to turn away but stopped when Marian said softly, 'Mart.'

She reached up and put her arms around his neck. She kissed him on the mouth.

He stood there for a moment, staring down at her. He started to ask her if this meant she had decided she would marry him, then changed his mind. He turned and crossed the street toward the Silver Dollar saloon.

Not many people in Medicine Lodge would sleep tonight, he thought. The saloons were all crowded. Every man he saw was armed. Some of the families who lived at the edge of town had left their homes and come to the hotel. Others had been taken in by friends who lived closer in.

He went into the Silver Dollar. He yelled, 'The Colfax place is under attack. I want some men to ride out there with me.'

The talk quieted in the saloon, but there were no volunteers. Mart yelled, 'This trouble isn't coming from the whole Cheyenne nation! It's only a few young bucks from the village of Angry Bear, but the more damage is done, the worse it's going to be later on.'

Only silence answered him. He turned in disgust and stamped out of the saloon. Most of the bunch that had wanted to lynch Max earlier tonight had been in there. His face twisted. They had guts enough for a lynching but not enough to face a few Cheyennes.

Furiously, he stamped across the street to Doc Williams' house. Taplow was carrying Otto out to the buggy. As he put the old man into it, Mart approached the buggy and looked at Otto's face. 'I want some of your men to go with me out to the Colfax place. Ben and Ed are holed up in the house and there are maybe half a dozen Cheyennes out there waiting for it to get light.'

'Why the hell should I help you?' The old man's voice was sour and uncompromising.

'Help me? Who said anything about helping me? I want you to help Ben and Ed. They're being attacked because of something your son did. If he hadn't killed Angry Bear . . .'

'How the hell do I know Max did it?'

'I saw him.'

Otto was silent for several moments, scowling bitterly, Mart could almost see the thoughts that were going around in his head through the changing expressions on his face. At last Otto said, 'All right, I'll give you three men.'

'And will you forget about breaking Max out of jail until I get back?'

Otto shrugged. 'Sure. Why not? The men are wore out anyway.'

Mart said, 'I'll get my horse,' and headed for

the jail where the two horses he and Marian had ridden in were tied. There was complete silence behind him, but he knew it would last only until he was out of hearing.

Otto had agreed to give him men, but Mart knew he hadn't done it out of the goodness of his heart. Mart was the only witness against his son. If Mart got killed . . .

He wondered if Otto would be able to talk any of the three men into shooting him. Probably not. He was probably just hoping that Mart would get himself killed by the Indians.

He reached the jail and stuck his head inside. 'When's Wortman coming back?'

'Daylight.'

'I'm going to the Colfax place again. Otto's loaned me three of his men, and he's promised not to try getting Max out until I get back.'

'What about that other bunch?'

'They're thinking about the defense of the town right now. I doubt if they'll bother you.'

Thorp shrugged. 'All right. I'll lock the door. I'm going to turn in pretty soon.'

Mart untied one of the horses and swung to his back. He rode back to Doc Williams' place where three of Gleason's men joined him. None of them spoke.

Mart knew this trip out to the Colfax place might be wasted time. Ben and Ed might still refuse to come in. If they did, he'd just have to flush the Indians out and drive them away.

It was thirteen miles from town to the

Colfax house. He raised his eyes and stared briefly at the position of the stars. He hadn't left town a bit too soon. They'd arrive just after dawn.

He pushed his horse as much as he dared and behind him, Gleason's three men kept pace. The hours slowly passed.

They were still a mile away when first gray began to touch the sky. They covered half that distance before they heard the shots.

At least, thought Mart as he stared into the grayness ahead of him, nothing had been burned. Not yet.

The shots came in a sudden volley, then settled down to a scattered popping of single reports. Mart sank his spurs and forced a sudden burst of speed from his weary horse.

Four abreast, they pounded down the narrow road and into the Colfax yard. From the house, both Ben and Ed began to yell. The Indians, seven in all, came flushing out of their hiding places like quail.

Mart hauled his horse to a halt. He yelled at Gleason's men, even though he realized it was no use. They pursued the seven Indians like executioners, and only three of the seven reached their horses and escaped.

Gleason's men might have gone after them, but Mart roared, 'Hold it! Let 'em go!'

The three rode back to him. Ben and Ed Colfax came from the house. 'What the hell's the matter with you, Mart?'

Mart shrugged wearily. He was tired of seeing men killed. He was tired of the way it pyramided, of the way it had all built out of a single steer shot with an arrow several days before. He said, 'Do you know how this started three days ago? Max found a steer with an arrow in it. Now Gleason's buildings are nothing but ashes and eight men are dead. Sam Farley's wounded and so is Frank Valenti.' He fished for his tobacco. 'Ben, how about hitching up a wagon for me? I'll haul these six bodies back to town and turn 'em over to Elvin Burke.'

Ben and Ed hurried across the yard to the barn. Mart finished his cigarette, threw it down, and stepped on it. He grinned at Jack Lane, the oldest member of Gleason's crew. 'Otto's going to be disappointed when he finds out nothing happened to me.'

Lane avoided his glance almost guiltily. Ben drove the wagon across the yard, and Mart followed it to where the Indians' bodies lay. He helped Ben load them up, then covered them with a tarpaulin. He said, 'How about driving, Lane?'

The oldster shrugged and tied his horse behind the wagon. He climbed to the seat and drove out toward town.

Mart glanced at Ben. 'I'll tell Marian that you and Ed are all right. Max's trial will be tomorrow. I've got an idea that the rest of the villages will wait until they see how that comes

181

out.'

He rode out, following the wagon. Otto Gleason's other two men followed him. And now, Mart just poked along, enjoying the warm sun on his back.

He had received some help—from Wortman and Thorp in guarding the jail—from Otto's men in driving the Indians away from the Colfax ranch. And yet he understood that when the showdown came, he would receive no help from anyone.

If Max was convicted, the Indians would be appeased, but Otto Gleason would fight to the death to save his son.

And if Max was not convicted—the Indians would fight, which would probably be much worse. Either way, it would be decided by tomorrow night.

CHAPTER NINETEEN

Medicine Lodge was tense when Mart reached it. Judge Billings had arrived on the train and had gone directly to the hotel. The troops had not yet arrived.

Mart had Jack Lane take the wagon to the livery stable and leave it there. He rode to the hotel to tell Elvin Burke what it contained.

The street was lined with wagons, driven into Medicine Lodge by ranchers who feared an uprising. They were loaded high with household goods, the things most prized by their owners who didn't know if they would ever see their homes again.

The saloons were filled to overflowing with townsmen, all of them armed, some of them drunk enough to be reckless and quarrelsome. Mart dismounted in front of the hotel.

He found Burke in the lobby, talking to Marian. He smiled reassuringly at her. 'Ben and Ed are all right. We drove the Cheyennes off.'

He turned his glance to Burke and said regretfully, 'Six of those Cheyennes are dead. I brought 'em to town in Ben's wagon. They're down at the livery barn, but it's cool down there. They'll keep until the troops get here.'

Burke's face sagged with discouragement. 'Couldn't you have . . . ?'

'Driven 'em off without killing 'em? Maybe, if I'd had anyone but Gleason's three men along with me. But I couldn't get help from anyone else in town. I had to take what I could get.'

Burke nodded. He stared at the floor between his feet. 'It's like watching an avalanche,' he said heavily. 'It's a long ways off when it starts and it doesn't look so dangerous, but as it comes closer it gets bigger and you know that nothing on earth will stop it.'

Mart said, 'Maybe this is no avalanche. Maybe if the court convicts Max Gleason, that will be an end to it.'

Burke nodded, but Mart could see he was not convinced. His expression was heavy with discouragement, and Mart realized he was thinking about returning the bodies of the young Indians to the village of Angry Bear—and dreading it.

Mart said, 'I'd better see Judge Billings.' He held Marian's eyes for a moment and she said, 'I'll go with you, Mart.'

He crossed the lobby to the desk, with Marian walking at his side. He got the judge's room number from the clerk and started toward the stairs. Marian, keeping pace with him asked, 'Are you sure Ben and Ed will be all right now?'

He nodded.

'And what about Max?' Her tone was neutral.

'I don't know. It will depend on who gets picked for the jury, I guess. The fact that Gleason's place has been burned isn't going to help. Neither is the fact that your place has been attacked. But if they turn Max loose—then it will take the Army to put the uprising down.' He could understand, suddenly, Elvin Burke's feeling of helplessness. He had the same feeling himself. He could not control what the jury did. He could only testify and if Max was found guilty, carry out the sentence of the court.

He left Marian at the foot of the stairs after

184

asking her to wait for him. He climbed the carpeted steps heavily. His leg ached and made him limp. He was hungry and felt as though he had not slept for days.

He went along the hall to the judge's room and knocked. The judge's voice called, 'Come in.'

He opened the door, went in, and closed it behind him. He said, 'Everything's ready, Judge. Do you want to start the trial at nine?'

Judge Billings nodded. His white hair was like a lion's mane above his darkly tanned face. His eyes were blue and penetrating. 'How's Sam?'

Mart grinned wearily. 'Last I heard he was holding his own. Doc thought he'd probably make it all right.'

'What about Otto Gleason?'

'If Max is convicted, he'll try and get him loose.'

'What kind of evidence have you got against Max?'

'An eyewitness. Me. I saw him kill Angry Bear.'

'That ought to do it. Can you hold Max if he is convicted?'

'I'll hold him, Judge.'

The judge studied his face for several moments. Then he nodded. 'All right, Mart. See you in court tomorrow.'

Mart went out the door and down the stairs to where Marian waited for him. He said, 'I'm

185

hungry. Let's go eat.'

She took his arm and squeezed it briefly, smiling up at him. Together they went into the hotel dining room.

*   *   *

The day dragged uneventfully past, as did the night. At dawn, a troop of cavalry from Fort McKinney rode up the main street of Medicine Lodge. They halted in front of the hotel while their commander talked to Elvin Burke briefly on the hotel veranda. Burke went back into the hotel, to reappear shortly afterward. He walked to the livery stable and a few moments later drove out sitting on the wagon that contained the bodies of the slain Cheyennes. Accompanied by a half dozen cavalrymen, he headed north toward the village of Angry Bear.

About half the troop began to set up a bivouac at the edge of town along the creek. The other half headed north toward the reservation, under a grizzled captain's command.

The streets began to fill. Mart Leathers walked to Mike Androvich's restaurant and got two trays, one for himself and one for Max. He returned to the jail.

Max was sullen and glowered at him as he put the tray down inside the cell. Mart said, 'Eat your breakfast, Max. Then I'll get the

186

barber for you if you want.'

'I'd rather shave myself.'

'All right. I'll bring a razor back to you.'

He returned to the office, sat down, and ate breakfast. He noticed that his hand shook slightly as he did.

Ruefully, he examined his own feelings. This was the morning of Max Gleason's trial. Mart realized that he wanted Max convicted, wanted him sentenced to die for his crime. He didn't exactly hate Max, he supposed, but the emotion he felt was pretty close to it. Max had abused and beaten Marian. He had wounded Sam Farley. He had killed Angry Bear. It didn't matter to Mart that fear had dictated his actions. It didn't matter why Max had done the things he had.

He finished his breakfast and shaped a cigarette. His hand still trembled as he lighted it. Even if the jury convicted Max and sentenced him to die ... it didn't mean he would. Otto Gleason wouldn't care how far he had to go to save Max's life. Mart couldn't get help from the cavalry in holding Max, either. This was a civil matter in which they would not intervene.

It would be up to him. He'd have to return Max to the jail after the trial without the help of anyone. He'd have to carry out the sentence and hang Max on the appointed day. He could not afford to let the townspeople help him do it, either. If he did, it might result in open warfare in the streets between the townspeople and Otto's crew.

He took a pan of warm water, Sam's razor, and shaving mug back to Max. He watched while Max washed and shaved. He took the pan, razor, and mug out of the cell. He cleaned himself up, then crossed to the window and stared outside. He thought of Marian. A change had been apparent in her last night. He knew she'd say yes if he asked her again to marry him. He'd ask her too. Tonight.

Already people were gathering up at the hotel. Medicine Lodge didn't have a courthouse. Trials were held in the hotel lobby because it was the biggest room in town. Mart looked at his watch. There was still an hour left to go.

The office door opened, and Wortman and Thorp came in. Both were uneasy, but their eyes were steady enough. 'Need any help?'

Mart shook his head.

'Otto isn't going to let you bring Max back here—not if the jury convicts him.'

'Maybe not.' He stared at the pair a minute before he spoke again. 'You two have been a lot of help. I appreciate it. But if I let you help now, it will mean tangling with Otto and his crew in the street. The whole town could get involved.'

'Maybe it's the town's business, Mart.'

Mart shook his head. 'It's the law's business.' He didn't say any more than that.

He wasn't even sure he could explain how he felt. He only knew that Sam Farley, had he been on the job, would have accepted no help from the people of the town. He guessed that he felt the same way Sam would have felt. Otto and Max Gleason had flung down a personal challenge to the law. They both had flaunted it and disregarded it. Through bringing Max to trial, the law was picking up the challenge they had so contemptuously thrown down to it.

Puzzled but obviously relieved, Wortman and Thorp went out and disappeared in the direction of the hotel. Mart looked at the clock. Only half an hour now.

He got up, crossed to the gunrack and got a double-barreled twelve-gauge down. He loaded it and stuffed a handful of shells into his pocket.

Out of the drawer of the sheriff's desk, he got the handcuffs and key. Dangling them from one hand, he went back to Max's cell. He unlocked it and went in. 'Turn around and put your hands behind you.'

Max obeyed sullenly and Mart snapped the handcuffs on. 'All right, let's go.'

Max walked ahead of him to the hotel. Mart stayed about three feet behind, the muzzle of the shotgun pointed at Max's back. He didn't see Otto, and he didn't see any of Otto's crew.

There was already a big crowd in the hotel lobby. Mart escorted Max to a chair and sat down beside him. Their entrance caused a momentary hush.

Max's face was white. His eyes had a trapped look to them. Mart's glance crossed the room and found Marian's face. Some of the marks Max's fists had put on it were still visible. He thought of Sam Farley, lying in bed at Doc's place, and he thought of Angry Bear, who had been killed for nothing more than escorting Marian home.

The judge entered the room, and everyone stood up. The trial began.

Selection of the jury took until almost noon. After that, the trial proceeded quickly. Otto had hired an attorney for Max, a former judge named Carter. His defense consisted of trying to prove Angry Bear wanted to kill Max because of the raid on his village, which Max had led.

Mart gave his testimony briefly, and quickly. Marian was called and testified that Angry Bear had escorted her home. The jury retired to an upstairs suite to deliberate.

Mart waited, the shotgun nearby. The crowd thinned as many of the spectators went home to eat.

Minutes crawled slowly past. Max grew increasingly nervous. At last, just before one o'clock, the jury came down the stairs.

The tension in Mart was now almost intolerable. He gritted his teeth and waited for the jury foreman to answer the judge's question, 'Have you reached a verdict?'

'We have, your honor.'

'How say you, guilty or not guilty?'

'Guilty, your honor.'

The judge looked at Max. 'Rise and face the jury.'

Max got up. Mart could see his knees trembling. The judge said, 'You have been found guilty of the crime of murder. Have you anything to say before I pronounce sentence?'

Max shook his head numbly.

Judge Billings said, 'It is the sentence of this court that you be hanged publicly at dawn of the 10th day of October, here in the town of Medicine Lodge.'

Mart's hands tightened slightly on the shotgun. He glanced around. A murmur ran through the courtroom. Judge Billings looked at Mart. 'Remove the prisoner, deputy.'

Mart nodded. 'Let's go, Max.'

Judge Billings rapped with his gavel. 'Spectators will remain seated until the deputy has removed the prisoner.'

Mart followed Max toward the door. Max stepped out into sunlight, and Mart said softly, 'This shotgun's cocked and pointed straight at your back. Don't make any sudden moves.'

Max turned his head. 'I didn't think they'd do it. This town don't like Indians any better than we do.'

'They were scared of 'em, Max. They were scared to turn you loose.'

'The yellow sons-of-bitches!'

Mart didn't reply to that. He was searching the street with his eyes. He didn't see Otto's buggy and he saw none of Otto's men. But he knew they would be there. Somewhere between here and the jail, they would be waiting for him.

He nudged Max with the shotgun muzzle. 'Head for the jail. If you try to run, I'll cut you in two. It's hard to miss with a twelve-gauge. You remember it.'

He glanced toward the jail. Right at this minute it seemed as though it was a hundred miles away.

Max moved out, his knees shaking, his eyes darting back and forth fearfully. A wry smile touched Mart's mouth. Right now, Max didn't know whether he wanted to see Otto or not.

Step by step, the pair proceeded toward the jail. Mart heard the clamor of voices behind him as the crowd streamed out of the makeshift courtroom in the hotel lobby. Max reached the first intersection.

Mart said, 'Hold it, Max,' and stopped his prisoner before he had stepped from behind the building corner. Cautiously he poked his head out and peered up the side-street.

He saw Otto's buggy almost instantly, saw the leveled rifle, and saw Otto's squinted eye behind the sights. He heard Otto bawl, 'Walk away, Max. Goddam him, I've got him in my sights!'

Mart said evenly, 'Go ahead, Max, if that's

what you think you've got to do. But you won't get to the middle of the street.'

Max froze, trembling from head to foot. He swung his head and looked imploringly at Mart. Mart said softly, 'All right then, we'll try it together.'

Mart raised the shotgun muzzle and poked it against the back of Max's neck. He said, 'Step ahead, Max. Easy does it now.'

Max stepped out into the intersection and Mart followed him. Without turning his head, he yelled, 'If you shoot, Otto, I'll get this trigger pulled before I fall.'

One slow step at a time, the two proceeded across the street. It was a guessing game now, Mart realized. Otto was trying to guess whether he would really pull the trigger, and he was trying to decide what Otto was going to do.

He hadn't long to wait. From Otto he heard a kind of enraged, wordless screech. He heard the snap of a whip and heard the pounding hoofs of Otto's buggy horse.

He risked a quick glance and saw Otto's horse galloping straight toward him less than a dozen yards away.

He had but a split second for decision. He could pull the trigger and blow Max's head off and instantly be killed himself. Or he could try and avoid the galloping hoofs of Otto's buggy horse.

The shotgun still rested against the back of

Max's neck. Mart gave the gun a violent push and saw Max fall forward, staggering from its force. He followed, scrambling frantically.

Instantly it seemed as though guns were roaring all up and down the street. A rifle bullet tore a furrow in the street behind Mart's feet and whined away into space. A revolver bullet tore the heel off one of his boots. But the buggy horse was past, and Otto was hauling back on the reins with a stream of savage profanities.

The horse reared between the shafts, and the buggy stood momentarily still. Otto tried helplessly to turn the animal.

Mart crawled forward to where Max lay. The firing had stopped as suddenly as it had begun. Now Otto's men were afraid they might hit Max.

Mart poked the shotgun against Max's body. He got slowly to his feet. The buggy was turning now. The horse had dropped to all four feet. Mart got a sudden glimpse of Otto's face.

It was wild with fury, completely out of control. Otto dropped the reins and swung the rifle in his hands. Its muzzle centered on Mart and steadied there . . .

Mart knew that Otto was going to shoot. Nothing would stop him now—not his son's mortal danger—not anything.

Forgetting Max for the moment, Mart flung himself aside, trying frantically to swing the shotgun barrel. The rifle in Otto's hands blasted, and the bullet seared Mart's ribs like a branding iron. He was falling, but his gun was coming into line . . .

He tightened his finger on the trigger the instant it did. He saw the full charge hit Otto Gleason in the face and chest. The man was driven back, his face obscured almost instantly by blood. The horse reared again, whirled as he came down, and galloped wildly down the street.

Mart's side burned fiercely. He crawled to Max and shoved the shotgun muzzle against him. 'Get up, you son-of-a-bitch!' he panted, 'and head for the jail. Your old man's dead and you will be too if anybody shoots at me again!'

A couple of horsemen pounded past him, pursuing the runaway buggy horse down the street. The rest of Otto's crew came from their hiding places and watched impassively, their guns hanging uselessly at their sides. Otto was dead and they all knew he was. There was no longer reason for them to fight Otto's battles or those of Otto's son. Mart watched as Max got to his feet and stumbled toward the jail.

It was over. Max would be hanged as soon as a scaffold could be built, and his death should satisfy the Cheyennes. Particularly since the cavalry was here in enough force to make further raids foolhardy.

He glanced back once and saw Marian running toward him from the direction of the hotel.

He prodded Max into the jail with the shotgun, followed him to his cell, and locked him in. He went back to the front office, reaching the door as Marian came in.

The answer he had wanted from her was in her eyes. It was the look every man seeks in the eyes of the woman who marries him. He put out his arms and for a moment held her tightly against his chest. When he bent his head her lips were raised and ready for his kiss.